WARNING!
THIS NOVEL IS CONTAGIOUS!

As the second selection of his *Discovery* series of previously unpublished books by new writers, 5-time Hugo winner, 2-time Nebula winner Harlan Ellison, quite literally the most honored writer in the world of imaginative literature, has come up with a remarkable book. A first novel by a 25-year-old fantasist named Arthur Byron Cover that combines the antic sense of Robert Sheckley, the far traveling of A. E. Van Vogt, the deadly serious wry whimsey of Kurt Vonnegut, and the examination of the human condition of Theodore Sturgeon with a fresh, invigorating talent all his own. It is the damnedest piece of writing you may encounter for a long time.

And *because* it is a strange, uncategorizable never-happened-before sort of book, the management (who edited DANGEROUS VISIONS and AGAIN, DANGEROUS VISIONS, so he ought to know *some*thing about picking good stories) warns you that you'll derive certain, uh, "benefits" from reading this novel: you will learn how mung is created, you will see at least two well-known sf authors satirized, you will visit the worlds of Snarf and Sharkosh (but not the nameless planet), and you will learn the exquisite value of role-playing in your life. You are also warned . . . this crazy book is contagious. You'll talk about it to your friends—and they'll rip it off! Beyond that, the management refuses to guarantee *any* damn thing!

AUTUMN ANGELS

Arthur Byron Cover

PYRAMID BOOKS ▲ NEW YORK

AUTUMN ANGELS

A PYRAMID BOOK, by arrangement with the Author, the Series Editor and the Author's Agent. This is an original novel and has never before been published in any form.

Pyramid edition published July 1975

ISBN 0-515-03787-7

Library of Congress Catalog Card Number: 75-15103

Printed in the United States of America

Pyramid Books are published by Pyramid Communications, Inc. Its trademarks, consisting of the word "Pyramid" and the portrayal of a pyramid, are registered in the United States Patent Office.

Pyramid Communications, Inc., 919 Third Avenue, New York, N.Y. 10022

Cover art by Ron Cobb

This novel is dedicated with love to the many historical and fictional characters herein lampooned, and to their creators. Both the creators and the characters have enriched my life. To Clint Eastwood and Sergio Leone; to Philip José Farmer, whose novels inspired and instructed me; to Robert Silverberg, who unwittingly provided me with my start; to Jeff Dowden, Fred Christian, Margie Feldmark, Randle Walsh, and Debbie Raymond; to David Wise, for providing me with source quotes; to my parents, Dr. William A. and Margaret Cover, who helped bankroll this operation during the two years it took to do the writing; to my brothers James, Bill and J. R.; and to my editor, Harlan Ellison, without whom this book would not have been written, and rewritten, and rewritten, and re. . .

ABOUT THE COVER ARTIST

This is RON COBB's first paperback painting. But—as readers of the Los Angeles *Free Press* have known for ten years—he is hardly a stranger to wide circulation and adoration of his artwork. For the ten or twelve shut-ins who have never encountered Cobb's work, be advised that his political cartooning is on that olympian peak where such as Jules Fieffer, David Levine, Robert Grossman, Ralph Steadman, Ronald Searle, Daumier, Herblock, Bill Mauldin, Thomas Nast and Feliks Topolski operate. His oft-reprinted and postered view of Los Angeles sliding into the Pacific has become a crash-pad favorite around the world. Three books of his razor sharp observations on the condition of our crumbling world have gone through many editions: RCD-25; MAH FELLOW AMERICANS; RAW SEWAGE. His extravagantly precise oil paintings sell to private collectors for staggering sums. He designed the space hardware for the film *Dark Star*. He is a madman.

Born 21 September 1937 in Los Angeles, he led a rich fantasy life as a child, in reaction to a life of boredom in Burbank. Anyone who has lived in Burbank will sympathize. He drew from the first time he learned which end of a pencil made the mess, and was a devotee of the EC Comic line. Through an association with the legendary "Chesley Donovan Science Fantasy Foundation," a semisatirical organization noted for the eccentricities of its members, who were intensely interested in the sciences and eventually the humanities, Cobb received his real education, traditional educational institutions having thrown up their hands in frustration.

He worked at the Disney Studios from 1955 to 1957 at the bottom of the animation hierarchy and from 1957 to late 1960 did odd jobs: assembly line, mailman, working on movie props. He was drafted into the US Army in 1961 and served till late in 1963. He is a vet of the Nam. From 1964 till the present, he has been a working artist—monster covers, album covers, logos, sf illustration—but it was not till his association began with the *Freep* that his work became popular worldwide. His work is syndicated weekly in over 90 newspapers. In 1970 he returned to full-time painting.

In mid-1972, on a lecture tour of Australia, he fell in love with the land of the koalas and took up residence for a year. He resumed his editorial cartooning for *The Digger*, a gadfly newspaper out of Melbourne and as a result went to Southeast Asia to make a "dramatized documentary."

Now back in LA, he has provided the DISCOVERY SERIES with its first cover coup, harbinger of future efforts by the editor to match the freshness of the series' writers with new artists.

THE φ Ψ Ω OF A B C

an introduction by
HARLAN ELLISON

I'll get to Cover in a moment. By the way, that's to be pronounced "*coe*-vuhr" not cover as in the sensational Ron Cobb cover of this book.

After the publication of the first title in this "Discovery" series, James Sutherland's STORMTRACK, the reviews began coming in and were, for the most part, highly complimentary; not just on the book itself, but on the entire concept of the series, for which many thanks. But one review in a sf fanzine titled *Gegenschein* gave me pause. I'd like to share the pause with you. After saying Sutherland's book was a good *Analog* type adventure and that it held together well for a first novel, the reviewer concluded with these remarks:

"Surprises. 1. This is very much a hard science story. 2. Ellison's introduction reads just like a normal introduction, and is entirely unlike a 'normal' Ellison introduction. Try it."

I paused, because I knew precisely what the reviewer meant, and I had to hang my head in ambivalence. Usually, when I'm writing one of these cow-catcher things, I get all wound up in the joy and wonder of the item I'm celebrating and I do have just the teensiest tendency to, uh, er, gallop off in three directions at once. But because I had wanted to preface the first "Discovery" title with as little hyperbole as possible, to indicate to readers of my work that these were serious books intended to stand on their *own* merits once they'd been abetted in their sale by the dubious value of my name, I laid back. Mellowed out, as they say. And so there wasn't too much lunacy and shouting. Just some sober comments on the series and what the program was intended to do, some rational remarks about the author, and a brief comment on the book itself. I'm afraid, friends, it was "normal." That is to say, it was understated.

I feel I may have gypped the readers who come to Ellison or Ellison-associated books expecting, if not the Second Coming, at least the San Francisco Earthquake, combined with the Sinking of Atlantis, the Eruption of Krakatoa, Noah's Flood, the Chicago Fire and the Last Days of Pompeii, scored for Quintaphonic sound, choreographed by Diaghilev, directed by Coppola, Altman, Fellini, Kubrick and Ken Russell all tied up in the same straitjacket and starring a cast of milions, no two alike or of the same sex.

Southerland's book was a ploy, of course. It was stalking horse of hard science, rational plotting and subdued theatrics, designed by your Machiavellian Editor to lull with a false sense of security those prone to Ellison derogation. No room left for haters of experimental writing to snarl, "That creep Ellison is at it again; busy polluting the mainstream of good old sigh-fie." Well, it served its purpose. Reviewers like the one quoted above smiled and commented on how mellow and down-to-earth it all was over her in Ellison Wonderland.

And having flummoxed them, here they are about to start reading the goddamedest, weird, wild, unbelievable, improbable, cockeyed, nutso, pervo-freako-devo novel I've come across in years of boredom in sf. Here, friends, right before your eyes, the editor runs amuck ranting and babbling about Cover and his eugenically-twisted offspring, AUTUMN ANGELS.

You want Krakatoa? You want the Flood? You want fire and brimstone and madness on a level never before witnessed by mundane humanity? Well, shucky-darn, have *I* got a book for *you*!

Which brings me to ABC. Arthur Byron Cover. Every phi/psi/omega inch of his warped brain. I met him at the 1971 Clarion Writers' Workshop in Science Fiction and Fantasy at Tulane University, New Orleans. I can describe Arthur with absolute fidelity. Go find a copy of the Marvel Comics version of *Thor*. At 5'7" that is Arthur. Not as brawny and muscular, of course, and considerably less heroic, but that's what Arthur looks like. Or, even better, pick up a copy of the DC Comic, *Kamandi*, drawn by Jack Kirby. There's this kid, see, with long straight blond hair and blue eyes and he looks like maybe something out of Booth Tarkington's PENROD AND SAM. Very clean-cut, aryan, not a doity thought in his head. That's Arthur. Except his head is full of some very tricky schmerz indeed. Like AUTUMN ANGELS.

I would probably have started off the "Discovery" series with Arthur's book, but two things stopped me. The first was that I wanted to begin with a quiet piece of work that wouldn't scare off old-line sf readers with all that freaky new stuff; the second was that Arthur did a lousy first draft.

"The "Discovery" series has to make it. It has to sell books, to enable other writers to get a place to break in. So I saved Arthur for second slot, till we had seen if the first book would earn its keep. Well, it did, and more. It sold very well, and Pyramid is happy; and we're moving on.

But before I move on, let me say a few things about *why* it's imperative that this series be successful.

When Silverberg and I broke into professional writing, about two years apart, in the early Fifties, we were the last of the pulp writers. We came in at the very flickering tail end of a great period for magazine writers. There were over thirty science fiction magazines alone, not to mention hordes of western pulps, detective and adventure books, pocket-sized fiction magazines and bedsheet-sized books like the *Post, Collier's,* and *Esquire*; every service magazine like *Redbook* and *Argosy* and *Cosmopolitan* published reams of fiction. And the men's magazines were just burgeoning. There were a hundred places to submit a story if it bounced out of the top markets. You could sell even the crap (and some of us sold a lot of it while learning our craft). Paperbacks like the Ace Doubles were publishing everything they could lay their hands on. It was a fine, fat time if you wanted to spend fifteen hours a day slumped over a typewriter.

Well, those days are gone. Dead and gone. Most of the magazines noted above are gone, killed by usurious postal rates, the increased desire on the part of the masscult reader for non-fiction of the "I Was the White House Gardener" sort, the paper shortage, the steady bastardization of taste of the American reading public through the hype of writers like Segal, Uris, Susann, Wallace and Robbins . . . a plethora of reasons. Suffice it to say the fiction magazines are one with the passenger pigeon, the cape lion and the quagga.

There are now a mere handful of sf magazines still managing to cling with bloody fingertips to the ledge of publishing solvency. And while they still publish more new fiction by first-time writers than any other genre of magazines, they can only do so much. As for the hardcover houses, well, with type and paper and printing costs soaring they can't indulge themselves too wildly with the works of even brilliant newcomers. Not when Jeb Stuart Magruder and the Thug Nixon have their memoirs to sell and slavering hordes of readers waiting to reward the criminals with more millions for the banal poop of their indiscretions. Paperback houses release hundreds of first-time novels every year, but with the nasty proliferation of brutality series like The Executioner, The Soul Sucker, Perry Rhodan, Cap Kennedy, Rack, Pinion and their ilk, all pap and an inch deep, there isn't much room on the stands to promote the hell out of a solid new talent.

And then, there's television, which has turned any number of generations from reading to mesmeric adoration of phosphordot inanities. Ah, but how I do go on. . .

The point is: a "Discovery" series, no matter how ineptly edited by someone like me, is a *necessary* thing; it is a noble cause. It will give all the Sutherlands and Covers and Marta Randalls and John Lawlesses a chance to write what they *want* to write, to get it out, to get it read, and—hopefully—to give a few more talented newcomers a chance to break in the way they should, with a showcase.

Bringing me back to Arthur Cover, whose "break-in" is infinitely more important, by my lights, than Harold Robbins' going deeper in debt with another bestselling turkey.

Arthur is twenty-five as I write this. He was born on 14 January 1950 in Grundy, Virginia. From 1954 to 1972 he lived in what he terms the heart of the White Trash Mountains of Virginia, in Tazewell. His father is a doctor, who used to be in general practice but finally wised up and became Director of the Health Department in Tazewell County so he could live on a salary. His mother studied to be a nurse for two years and then packed it in so she could, as Arthur puts it, "be a housewife and raise four weird sons." Didn't help; she has spent years in Dad's office, licking stamps, telling cripples they can see the Doctor now, and hemstitching leaky patients.

Weird Arthur—who affects a cornball Suth'n accent so everyone will think he's a brain damage case and won't beat the crap out of him when he's smartass—graduated from Tazewell High School and from Virginia Polytechnic Institute and State University; the BA is in English, a language Arthur has set his talents to eviscerating, clearly out of a sense of frustration at its complexities.

Freak Arthur discovered *Flash Comics* when he was ten and Edgar Rice Burroughs when he was thirteen. Beyond these two seminal influences, Arthur has never made even a nodding acquaintance with the world of literature. As this novel will demonstrate, literature made a hairbreadth escape.

Strange Arthur sold me his first story. It's called "Various

Kinds of Conceits" and it's scheduled for publication in THE LAST DANGEROUS VISIONS when the final volume of the DV trilogy is published by Harper & Row, around Christmastime this year . . . God and my typing fingers willing. Since that first sale Odd Arthur has sold a dozen articles and stories to a wide range of publications. He has also sold this novel. You have bought it. One of you is in trouble.

Now we get to the novel itself.

Did you know that William Morris designed and manufactured the first Morris chair in 1866 and that this adjustable reclining chair was so enormously popular and widely copied that it became virtually omnipresent in late Victorian England and America? Did you know that? Did you know that the term "Morris chair" now denotes a chair, usually made of oak, whether or not made by Morris and Co., with a bar-and-notch arrangement to adjust the tilt of the back to about a 45°angle; with flat, wide upholstered arms and a large, usually loose, cushion for the back and one for the seat? Did you know that?

You're probably wondering why I'm telling you all this. Read AUTUM ANGELS and you'll see why I thought you should know about it. You'll also understand why, though I don't *personally* subscribe to the deranged philosophy of the ending, I do feel it is consistent within the mad parameters of the novel's equation. You'll also understand why it's interesting but not imperative that you know the pig Shadwell is modeled after Thomas Shadwell, the late 17th century poet whom Dryden lampooned in "Mac Flecknoe."

You see, AUTUMN ANGELS is not your usual tacky *tour de force* practically gavaged with symbolism till it bursts at the binding. It is almost entirely free of symbolism. In point of fact, it manages to dispense with many of the sordid necessities of lesser novels; *dreck* like plot, movement, theme, structure, metaphor, index, table of contents, rationality.

AUTUMN ANGELS is a *rara avis;* or, in line with the

tone of the work, it is a crawling bird. It is also a wander through the chill corridors of Carter Hall where the last relics of old Earth are stored; it is a box seat at the telepathic power struggle of two godlike men as they try to exile each other to the anti-matter universe; it is an eyewitness as the demon, the fat man (not the *other* fat man) and the lawyer—standing straight up—travel eight million light-years per second through outer space. It is a great many things, most of them silly and funny and memorable.

It is the game of "who is that supposed to be." But unlike cheap contemporary novels in which the thin disguises always mask someone like Judy Garland or Elizabeth Taylor or Sammy Davis, Jr., AUTUMN ANGELS is jammed through with wild characters from a pop culture/nostalgia buffs scrapbook:

For instance: the lawyer is modeled after Doc Savage's sidekick, "Ham," Brig. Gen. Theodore Marley Brooks; the fat man is Sidney Greenstreet; the gunsel is Elisha Cook, Jr. in *The Maltese Falcon;* the Big Red Cheese is Captain Marvel; the Insidious Oriental Doctor is Fu Manchu; the Queen of England who calls herself a virgin is Elizabeth I; the ace reporter is Lois Lane; the zanny imp from the Fifth Dimension is Mr. Mxyzptlk, and both the imp and Lois are, of course, from the *Superman* comics; the godlike man with no name is Clint Eastwood in the Sergio Leone-directed spaghetti westerns; the galactic hero with two right arms is Harry Harrison's BILL, THE GALACTIC HERO; the fuzzy (but boring) little green balls of Sharkosh are *Star Trek* scenarist David Gerrold's tribbles; and you can figure out for yourself the true identities or esoteric references for The Ebony Kings, the poet, the shrink, the bems, the other fat man and his witty leg man, and on and on.

But though AUTUMN ANGELS is the kind of delicious book over which you can cackle because of the private jokes, even thought it's a kind of game book, there comes a moment when the fun ceases and you—as I—must stop to consider the deeper values of its seemingly pointless ramblings. For me, in this introduction, the moment is now, and

I will take this moment to explain to you why I think AUTUMN ANGELS is a very fine, very important book.

For openers, it is what Charles Dickens called a "moreeffoc novel." That is a word brought to us from Dickens, via G. K. Chesterton, by way of the fantasy historian and brilliant editor, Lin Carter. As Lin advises us in the introduction to a Chesterton novel, "When as a poor child, Dickens slaved in the dismal captivity of that firm he later portrayed with chilling and gruesome detail, as 'Murdstone and Grinby,' he saw this weird mystery-word through a grimy window. What did it mean? What *could* it mean? Obviously, it meant nothing at all. Obviously it *must* mean something.

"The baffling mystery at length was solved. The weird glyph yielded up its secret meaning. The child had been looking at a mirror image of a sign painted on a window. He had been reading it backwards, or from the opposite side. 'Mooreeffoc' simply meant 'Coffee-room.' There was nothing mysterious or cryptic about it at all . . . *unless you looked at it from the wrong angle*.

"When you look at common, everyday reality *from the other side*, the ordinary and the commonplace undergo a remarkable transformation; the difference between the fantastic and the mundane lies in your point of view. Reality, seen from a fresh perspective, becomes unbelievable and bizarre."

And so, AUTUMN ANGELS is a "mooreeffoc novel." It takes the materials of everyday entertainments—pulp heroes, movies, comics, detective stories—and transforms them. It melds them into a gestalt that is fresh and different and entertainingly meaningful. Despite my cutting-up in this introduction, make no mistake: I take AUTUMN ANGELS and its brilliant young author *very* seriously. It is, as you will discover somewhere in its middle sections, a peculiarly moving piece of work. The crawling bird, the eternal children, the lonely hawkman . . . they each have a surprising ability to make lumps come to the throat. And despite the seeming silliness of the story, it is a profound and singular examination of some of the basic questions that confound us today: the meaning of our existence, the value of pain, the rationale for the search for individual destiny. And AUTUMN ANGELS speaks directly to the act of role-playing in our society; it says something lucid and fresh about the value of our persona, the need to be other than what we seem, the need to seem to be other than what we are. I do not take these questions lightly nor, under the clown makeup, does the book. Arthur Cover has chosen a cakewalk as the style, but the dance is the stately pavane of life.

And so, through jabberwocky and hi-jinks, both Arthur Cover and I have tried to lead you. He to entertain and make the message as painless as possible, I to get you to read what I take to be an important first venture by a remarkable talent. Do not let our japery mislead you. We are both dead serious, the way "mooreeffoc" is a serious business at core.

And to bolt it down, so you labor under no misconception, permit me to say that if the "Discovery" series were to go no further, I would take it as a worthy project simply because I was able to find and put before you this wonderful, funny, heartbreaking, insane, dead serious novel of antic spirits and wry delusions. As they say when they make pompous speeches, I'm proud to have had a hand, however slight, in getting AUTUMN ANGELS published.

I hope you will pay close attention to this book, tell your friends about it, and watch for further writings from ABC, the phi/psi/omega writer, Arthur Byron Cover.

HARLAN ELLISON
Los Angeles
6 April 75

CHAPTER ONE

1. It was early morning; orange sunlight broke through yellow clouds, and the jungle, forgotten by all but two godlike men, came to life again. The jungle: red trees, black apes, golden singing snakes wrapped around weak, crooked limbs. The jungle: on a planet five thousand square kilometers large, with a core so dense its life and atmosphere could not fly off into space. Mere man would have called it a miracle, but it was much less than that. It was a toy; it had cost a lone godlike man five hours' labor.

The demon sat in the air. He allowed the wind currents to take him anywhere. He looked down, angry that the object of his search had eluded him for several minutes. The demon was five meters tall; he had four nostrils and he did not have a nose; instead of a mouth he had a beak. He reached down with a thin green arm and fondled the huge penis hanging below his folded legs. He had four white nipples, yellow eyes, and long red fingernails that looked as if they would break should he scrape something; but they never did. He did not have joints in his fingers. His toes were three orange birdlike claws. (Yet his appearance was not repulsive; it was fascinating. Godlike men could not help but stare as he floated past them, and as he noticed them staring at him, silently acknowledging his daring imagination, he felt a warm glow of pride and confidence which convinced him that it was his duty to shape the destiny of others.)

The lawyer materialized beside the demon. He tipped his

black derby at his friend. He was a meter and a half tall; he carried a sword-cane; he wore a red vest, a ruffled white shirt, and a black suit with a plastic flower in the lapel. He twirled his sword-cane and said in a nasal voice, "I found one. I believe the others are underground, trying to make a new life for themselves."

"You mean they're underground so they won't have to look at the sky." The demon rubbed his hands.

"Yes, that's what I mean. *You* know and *I* know it won't make much difference, but *they* don't know it yet."

"Now that's funny," said the demon. "It just breaks me up. I can see them now, looking at the ceilings in the caverns and wondering, as they wondered out here, how they can get up. Will they think they're crippled bats? Will they think their purpose is to hang upside down?"

"There are bats in the caves. They'll look at themselves and they'll see they're different from bats."

"Perhaps the more intelligent will," said the demon, turning his head one hundred and eighty degrees to look at the cliffs behind him. "You must remember that most of them are, by our admittedly high standards, retarded."

The dapper young lawyer created a lit cigarette and puffed at it. "Perhaps, friend demon, perhaps. I don't know." He paused, a sudden smile coming to his face. "Did you know there are pigs here?"

"Really?"

"Big fat ones, with long pink quills instead of hair, but pigs nevertheless. They have orange eyes and snouts so large and so heavy they can't lift them from the mud. I killed four of them and watched the others try to run away."

"I'm not surprised."

"That I killed four?"

"No. That they find it difficult to run with such huge snouts. If you had not killed any, I would have been disappointed in you." He started to say something else, but a hasty gesture from the lawyer interrupted him.

"I don't want to hear another joke about my hating pigs and what my birthright has to do with it." The lawyer grimaced. Normally his handsome features, his high cheekbones, his wide, smiling mouth, his blue eyes, and his short black hair made him appear to be twenty-five years old; his skin was smooth and pale; his lips were thin and very red. But when he grimaced he looked as if he were twenty years older.

"All right, but *that* makes me disappointed in you."

"Nothing new."

"Which doesn't make it right. You should be tough-skinned by now. I don't complain when people joke about my peenie."

"They joke from envy, not from distrust and dislike."

"Some of them distrust and dislike me."

"They envy you, too," said the lawyer. "Let's find our bird."

2. A crawling bird rested at the precipice. His tiny, darting eyes surveyed the treetops below. He whimpered; something inside him wished he could fly to the singular tree that had grown twice as tall as the rest, almost parallel to the edge of the precipice.

The godlike man who had built the jungle eons ago had given him the instinct to fly; he did not understand what flying was, nor did he understand why he felt empty and useless; he only knew he wanted to spend hours looking at the yellow clouds and wishing he could be close to them, feeling their mist on his wings, and looking at the treetops, seeing them from above. His plumage, save for his red wings, was deep blue; his brittle beak and claws were yellow. The only hunger he felt was to fly; he desired few insects and worms. He could neither hop nor walk; his legs hung uselssly behind him. His wings were equipped with primitive appendages used to grasp rocks and stumps, and to drag him in the direction he wished to go. Because the ground he ususally crawled over was covered with sharp pebbles and thorns, his belly was matted with mangled feathers, blood, and broken scabs.

For the first time in his life the crawling bird was alone in his misery. The collective intelligence of his kind had discovered a possible cure for their suffering, and the crawling birds had left the surface for the caves. He had once had a mate, and the closest they had ever known of peace was their mutual consolation. They had sung to each other, trying to forget the incomprehensible desire which haunted and pained them. Now he had no one to sing to but himself; and he did not know if he would receive any comfort from that.

Not knowing what else to do, he sang. The golden snakes in the forest below heard his hideous wailing, and they were angry because one crawling bird could sing louder than a hundred of their kind. The snakes fought back in the one way they could, by singing their songs of evil. The crawling bird heard their song underneath his and, shocked, he stopped singing. The snakes laughed at him; he could hear them even though he was far above them. Their laughter grew louder and louder as his silence lengthened. The bird had no desire to sing if the snakes were to be his only audience. He wondered what else there was for him to do. He had to do *something* to stop the gnawing inside him.

He crawled down the path leading to the jungle. He whimpered, no longer able to ignore the pain caused by the pebbles and thorns. He halted, realizing he had been crawling too fast. He felt fortunate that he could not lift himself and bend his neck to look at the wounds on his belly. He groped toward a sapling and pulled himself toward it; he would take his time now.

The crawling bird looked up, intending to gaze at a yellow cloud, and saw instead the demon hovering above him. He whimpered; something inside, something which did not quite communicate to him, was envious of this strange new creature. He reached toward the demon and whimpered again. He realized that no matter how hard he tried, he could never touch the demon.

He stared at the creature wrapped in black that was materializing beside the demon. He whimpered. He tried to understand their language, or anything about them, and could not.

"Do you think he suits our purposes?" asked the lawyer, flicking away his cigarette. The cigarette landed beside the crawling bird, who backed away from it.

"Indeed I do. He'll have to be cleaned up. And look at the trail of blood he's left behind him. Oh well, that won't take much effort."

"Then we take him to Earth?" The lawyer twirled his sword-cane.

"Yes, yes. No question about it."

And they took the crawling bird to Earth, home of the godlike men.

3. The crawling bird found himself in a silver-walled apartment adorned with paintings of scenes from Hell.

Each painting had been signed with a pentacle by the demon. One depicted a lovely woman kneeling in front of the devil; the devil bent over to touch her breast; his erection touched her stomach; a troll knelt between her legs and drank torrents of blood. Another depicted trolls' delight in scurrying over the devil's throne; they ignored the fires burning their heads. A third illustrated a minstrel singing to the devil's mate, a medusa with tremendous breasts that sagged below her navel. Yet a fourth, the most puzzling of all to the crawling bird, was of a huge black bat crashing into a cavern wall and of trolls and witches laughing at it.

The bird was filled with a disquiet he could not understand. Finally he could look at the paintings no longer. He crawled to a corner, delighted by the sensation of the furry rug on his belly. He noticed that for the first time in his life his belly was cured, whole. He did not feel whole inside, but at least it was good to feel whole outside.

The bird wanted to study the two creatures who had brought him here. He wanted to understand them or their language, though he doubted he could. There was nothing to do but watch them and feel the gnawing inside.

The lawyer twirled his sword-cane; he stopped when the cane almost hit and shattered a glass statue of the demon sitting on an ebony pedestal. "This is a cheery place," he said.

The demon snorted. "It's better than the bright world outside. The only reason I have green bedspreads is to remind me of dead babies. I need some contrast in my life. Do you want something to drink?"

The lawyer sat in a Morris chair and rested his sword-cane on his lap. "Lemonade, if you please."

21

The demon conjured a glass of lemonade into the lawyer's hands and then sat in the air, folding his legs and making sure his penis was comfortably dangling below. He stared at the crawling bird cowering in the corner. He rubbed the tip of his beak, pricked his finger, and watched the black pus oozing from the cut; it welled up, he turned the finger over, the pus formed a tear and fell, making a spot on the rug.

"I wonder," said the lawyer, sipping his lemonade.

"About what?"

"About this creature. I wonder just how much he understands. He appears to inspect everything, no doubt searching for a clue to the meaning of his existence."

"Right now he's inspecting the light fixture," said the demon. "In that respect he's like a moth."

After finishing his lemonade and causing the glass to disappear, the lawyer said, "That doesn't answer my question."

"I didn't know it was a question."

"A speculation."

"Well, to answer your speculation," said the demon, "I say he probably understands very little. And he'll understand even less when we're finished with him." The demon paused. "Something else to drink?"

The lawyer burped, belatedly covering his mouth with his fingertips. "No, thank you."

"To whom shall we show him first? On what segment of godlike humanity will he have the most effect?"

"Eternal children, if they weren't artificial, immature brats."

"Women, if they weren't quickly given to pity."

"Poets?"

"Executive types?"

The lawyer drummed his fingers on his sword-cane. "We do have a problem. And our problem is that we have a probable solution and no way to use it."

"Something like that," said the demon.

"We need help," said the lawyer, pressing a button and looking at the silver tip of his sword. "We need help desperately."

"We've reached a moment of indecision. Very bad for godlike men with hobbies such as ours."

22

The lawyer pressed another button and the blade withdrew into the cane. He opened his mouth and stared at the demon. His blue eyes were wide and full of fear. "What about the fat man?"

The demon drew back in shock. "The fat man?"

"Can you name a better ally, one more respected by the dull, unthinking masses? Can you name someone else who is more a manlike god than a godlike man? A more gifted master of intrigue? A more imposing figure? Think of how much help he could give us! Why, even his tactful approval would set forces in motion which . . ." The lawyer's voice trailed off; he was deep in dreams of ambition.

The demon scraped the dried pus from his finger with his beak. "But there will be nothing in it for him. There's certainly nothing in it for us."

"Only satisfaction and hope if we succeed. The fat man needs no hope, but he loves to be satisfied."

"I don't know if he will want to work with us," said the demon, causing his finger to heal. "I have my doubts. He cares nothing for my beloved appearance of evil and sorcery; he cares nothing for my life-style." He caused the spot on the rug to vanish.

"He has a grudging respect for you."

"But he *admires* you, friend lawyer, as he showed when he bailed you out of that despicable affair with Kitty last year. If we got to him, you must do the talking."

"He cares for my schemes, but he cares nothing for my talking," said the lawyer.

"That's true. Your voice does grate on the nerves. If your voice became more piercing, one could crucify oneself on it."

The lawyer flushed. He lifted himself four inches from the Morris chair and pointed a thin finger at the demon. Before he could reply there was a knock on the door. Immediately forgetting his anger, the lawyer said, "That sounds like a fateful knock. Do you want me to answer it?"

"It would be nice."

The lawyer opened the door and the fat man entered, taking off his large white Borsalino and tossing it on the golden hat tree shaped like the ancient demon Behemoth, an elephant who walked on two legs, who had a tremendous round stomach and hands with six claws. The Borsalino landed on one tusk and spun about; on the other tusk was the lawyer's derby.

"The fat man!" exclaimed the lawyer.

"The fat man!" exclaimed the demon.

The crawling bird was frightened by the arrival of this new, imposing figure. Although he had understood nothing the demon and the lawyer had said, something inside had hinted that he was the pawn in a childlike game. He sensed that the fat man had suddenly endowed the game with a sinister aspect. He had hoped to somehow comprehend the events swallowing him; he now knew he never could. He pushed himself tighter into the corner and hoped the fat man would ignore him. He shivered, wanting to whimper or sing. The gnawing inside became worse, much worse, and the bird wished he could look again at an orange sun and yellow clouds.

The fat man smiled, showing four gold teeth and a tongue wriggling like the tail of a snake. "You are surprised to see me? You should not be. My gunsel is everywhere and he informed me that you have a proposition to make."

The fat man patted his great bulk, admired the lawyer's sword-cane, and took off his white gloves. He was dressed completely in white except for his black tie and grosgrain leather spats. He was balding and had deep green eyes that suggested he had no compassion anywhere in his heart. His eyes were not deceptive. He looked down at the lawyer. "I realize that Morris chairs are your favorites, but they are mine also. If it will not offend you—?"

"Of course not," said the lawyer. "Sit down."

The fat man did, crossing his thick legs at the ankles and pulling his trouser cuffs over his white socks. "I have a grudging respect for you, demon. I always have a grudging respect for someone whose schemes are not concerned with fame and/or glory. Unlike you, I believe that the best way for a godlike man to serve the devil is to ignore him. That is all he deserves——and you keep your immortal soul in the bargain. Speaking of bargains, what of this proposition?"

The lawyer opened his mouth and the demon opened his beak at the same time, but before either could speak, the fat man silenced them with a gesture. "One at a time, please. I deplore eagerness." He noticed for the first time the crawling bird in the corner. He smiled and pointed. "May I suspect that your proposition has to do with this rather emotional creature?"

"You may do more than suspect, friend fat man," said the demon. "You see, we don't have exactly a proposition, but we're asking for advice. We want the masses to see him and learn from him."

The fat man steepled his sausage fingers. "Learn what?"

"Depression," said the lawyer.

"Depression. There has been none of that since the old days. Disappointment, dissatisfaction, yes, but no genuine depression. Everybody is happy; which is as it should be. You two are not living in the past, are you?"

"I disagree with your views," said the demon. "Without depression, what good is happiness? These days happiness is no longer a goal, but merely another state of being. As for myself, I find no joy in seeing other people happy. The race of godlike man has become lazy. The only ambition is for fame and glory. There is no striving for unobtainable goals. There are no adventures. And may I remind you that our very identities come from the past? Why shouldn't they come from our own culture, our own present? And what is our future?"

The fat man rubbed one of his chins. "I do not care for your goals. I, for one, am completely satisfied with things as they are."

"And for eons," said the lawyer, "you have been concerned with petty intrigues. Why, a man with your skills in the old days would have fought and schemed for a planet, for a solar system, for more! Your skills are wasted on this dreamless planet. With the return of depression will come the return of dreams, of hopes for better times. All godlike men will be searching for something, and then your skills will not be wasted. You will be at the top of a young and worthwhile race."

"You would appreciate my wife," said the fat man. "She has hinted as much to me, but she is very dull and stupid. You two are bright and philosophical; you express things directly. I like directness; I like the way you two come right to the point. It is as if you are running out of time."

"I assure you," said the demon, "we have all the time in the world."

"Don't we all?" The fat man stood up with difficulty and pointed at the bird. "An unusual creature. I am the only one who could possibly be unaffected by its predicament. I think I can help you."

"How?" asked the lawyer.

The fat man put on his gloves and retrieved his Borsalino. He admired an ivory lamp carved in the shape of a voluptuous mermaid. He walked to the door and turned around. "We shall hold a carnival, a rodeo, a fair. There has not been one for centuries. The crawling bird will be our main attraction."

"And what is your price?" asked the demon.

"One hundred per cent of the fame and glory." He closed the door gently behind him.

4. Dawn came to the Earth of the godlike men. It was a dawn no less grand than the millions that had preceded it, with a golden sun streaking its rays like spiderwebs across a limpid azure sky, with dew dripping from green and red and purple bushes, from the golden gutters of golden buildings, with a few godlike men rubbing their eyes and readying themselves for pursuit of their hobbies. Trees, each a kilometer tall, ran in straight lines to the horizon. Flying squirrels—created by the demon, in fact, so they could live up to their name—flew from tree to tree, collecting nuts and berries. It was neither too hot nor too cold; it was, simply, just perfect.

On Earth, *everything* about a new day was perfect and picturesque.

Most people did not know that: they had the pleasure of sleeping late if they chose.

Today, the new dawn had come up on something different. It caused the few early risers to smile and slap their knees and kiss their spouses. They said, "The fat man, bless his immortal soul, has done it again!"

They became as children again and ran to their parents to wake them. Their cranky parents did not care what joyous news their real children had brought them. The parents dismissed their children and drank orange juice. They looked out the window and forgot all about their crankiness. They said, "It's just like the old days! The doing of the fat man, eh? Well, it's to be expected."

The portly author who liked to hunt and fight in wars rubbed his beard and smiled. There would be new experiences to write about.

The Queen of England who called herself a virgin (but had lost the right to use that designation at the age of thirteen) concealed her pleasure in a royal way. She could take a day off from listening to the complaints of her beloved subjects.

The superhero who had saved Earth a thousand times said the magic word and leaped over a tall building at a single bound.

The insidious Oriental doctor forgot to toy with an infernal machine.

The poet who had always yearned for the return of childhood, for the first time truly felt the wonder of a child. He combed his wavy white hair, wrote a poem, and then made plans to personally congratulate the fat man.

What the godlike men had seen was the skywriter indulging in his hobby. He flew his Fokker triplane with a wild abandon. But what he wrote was the important thing:

TAKE FAT MAN PRESENTS A FAIR!
BASEBALL, GAMBLING, AND FREAKS!
FERRIS WHEELS AND A THOUSAND OTHER RIDES!
AND THE WONDER OF THE AGES:
!!THE CRAWLING BIRD!!

Nobody could wait, but the fat man told them they would have to. The big day finally came and they, holding the hands of eternal children, went to the fair.

They saw cowboys in red plaid shirts wrangling winged broncos. The cowboys fell twenty meters and landed on their bottoms and shook their fists at the horses hovering above them. Clowns laughed at the cowboys and, using skyhooks, chased the horses back into the corral.

They saw the three-legged man from Nefarious X who could dodge anything. The freak laughed at them as they threw peanuts at him. He laughed at them until the spaceman got mad and threw a pebble from a dwarf star at him.

Its gravity pulled him into orbit around it and crushed him till he was a drippy mass. Before any more damage could be done, the gunsel, right-hand servant of the fat man, whisked the pebble into the anti-matter universe and banished the spaceman from the fair at gunpoint.

They saw the four dancing sirens from the edge of the galaxy. The sirens wore quivering algae and hushpuppies. The sirens did not sing; they merely opened their mouths. The godlike men were captivated by a droning noise washing over them, comforting them, soothing them. The song the godlike men heard was what they *wanted* to hear, and they heard infinite loveliness, secret passions, the merging of souls. The sirens did not dance; they merely moved their hands. The godlike men saw what they *wanted* to see, and they saw epics reenacted, past and future loves coming together, birth after death. The godlike men were humbled, awed by the beauty they thought they had seen and heard. When the dancing sirens concluded their act, the godlike men sat in silence, too overcome to demand "More!"

And they rode the ferris wheel that whirled through complex configurations of time; they saw the sun explode and the birth of the Earth, flickering colors against the black of space, their pasts and futures, their triumphs. Carousels traveled at the speed of light and took them to worlds in other galaxies; when the ride ended, the godlike men, used to such things, were not even dizzy and they laughed at the blurs they had seen. They rode an octopus that was a real live giant octopus. And they rode many other rides which astounded, amazed, and amused them. They always went back for more.

They saw the parade of the Ebony Kings, Negro villains who had conquered the worlds of other solar systems and had allied themselves against the forces of good. They all looked alike—five meters tall, with shiny bald heads and with small eyes darting back and forth. They wore purple robes lined with white lace. They carried scepters with living, intelligent devils' heads that spat and cursed at the audience. The Ebony Kings marched across the stage and ignored the sweat dripping from their faces; their postures were perfect. It had not taken much for the fat man to convince the Ebony Kings to humiliate themselves as objects in a sideshow; it had taken only a minor display of his awesome power.

The fat man watched them in satisfaction. He smiled and tipped his white Borsalino at them. "A fine job you are doing, my good men. My gunsel likes you, too. I do not know if he will require your services later on, but do not worry; the pleasure will be all yours. I believe I will let you keep your tiny worlds, at least until I need them at a later date. Again, do not worry; you will most likely be dead by then. Keep up the good work." The fat man turned to the demon and the lawyer. "Is it going nicely?"

If a godlike man with a beak could smile, the demon smiled. "I like it."

The lawyer twirled his sword-cane. "I haven't had so much fun since the last time I saw Kitty." He paused. "By the way, did you know there are pigs here?"

The fat man pondered the statement. "Do not worry. I bought them off."

"That's not what I meant," said the lawyer. "I mean the yellow pigs from the North Pole. With the corkscrew tails and the trench coats. They're really nice people, considering they're such retarded animals."

"I wonder if the yellow pigs will like our crawling bird," said the demon. "I wonder if the people are ready for what we're offering."

"I think they are," said the lawyer.

Smiling, slowly closing his eyelids as if their weight were too much for him to bear, the fat man rested his huge hands on his stomach. "I have had enough fame and glory for the night."

5. The crawling bird did not know how long he had been imprisoned in the little cage with the gold top and bottom and with bars of glowing yellow light; he had no criteria to judge the passing of time. He did know that the gnawing inside was undiminished. A violet sheet covered the cage, concealing his surroundings. Once he touched the bars of light in an attempt to learn more, or to escape (he was never sure which), and he felt an electric shock that sent him scurrying to the center of the cage. Although the shock actually hurt no worse than the gnawing inside, it seemed even more forceful and piercing. At least it died quickly; the other pain always remained.

Sometimes he thought of the demon sitting in the air. He could sense (but never form the thought fully) that sitting in the air approximated what he wanted. Often he whimpered for hours, never sure why, but knowing the demon was involved. The bird wished he could communicate with the demon. But how? The bird and his mate had once established a rapport through singing and mutual pain; the demon, as far as the bird could sense, had never experienced true pain.

Suddenly the crawling bird felt his atoms painlessly breaking up and speeding to another place. When he arrived where the fat man had sent him (for surely the sinister godlike man was the cause), the cage still held him prisoner, but he sensed he would soon be free. Again, he had no conception of his surroundings. He felt strangely calm, believing he would soon receive the answers he wanted so desperately.

He heard rustlings. Some were distant; others were close. They encircled him. They multiplied slowly and steadily. The bird wondered about their source. He felt a weight which did not hurt but made him anxious. Something needed to be done, and he wanted it finished quickly.

The fat man pulled the sheet from the cage and casually tossed it behind him. The bird saw a million godlike men staring at him. His first impulse was to look away; he looked to his right and saw a million more. There were a million to his left and a million at his back. They were all mysterious and unusual, incomprehensible; there was not one identical with another. They smiled and laughed and talked. Some sat with their arms folded, others with their hands on their laps, and others with ther hands under their buttocks. Whispering to their neighbors, some pointed at the crawling bird, dwarfed by the fat man and the stage. The fat man bowed, and the audience applauded (except for the Queen who nodded to show her royal pleasure), deafening the crawling bird.

"Hurrah for the fat man!" the people screamed. "Hurrah! Hurrah! Hurrah!"

"We are amused," murmured the Queen. The fat man beamed, took off his great white Borsalino with a sweeping gesture, and bowed again. He stood up straight, holding out his arms, asking for silence. The godlike men immediately complied.

"Thank you, my dear godlike friends," said the fat man. "Thank you for all the fame and glory you have given me. I must have more than anybody else by now! Thank you! Thank you!"

The people applauded louder than before. The fat man strutted back and forth on the stage, his hands in his coat pockets, his gold teeth reflecting light back at the audience. Finally he held his arms upward, and the people were suddenly quiet.

"But I cannot take all the credit for this magnificent fair!" he said. "True, I deserve most of it, but the demon and the lawyer are responsible for the greatest attraction of all. I realize you do not now understand, so I will explain. Generous of me, eh?

"You see caged beside me the crawling bird. The demon and the lawyer found him, and they know more about him than any other godlike man. Which is very little. We want you to watch him perform and, most of all, we want you to learn from him. I assure you, this will be the greatest moment of your lives!"

The people applauded. They were not applauding the bird, but the fat man's speech. The fat man held up his arms and said, "In a few seconds I will walk off this stage. Though I realize you feel you must, do not applaud my exit. At the moment the crawling bird is the most important thing. Please sit in silence, watch him, and learn from him."

The fat man strutted off the stage and sat between the demon and the lawyer in the front row. The confused godlike men were silent. They could not understand what they were supposed to learn while watching the crawling bird. The four sirens dressed in algae had not taught them anything. Nor had the ferris wheel whirling through complex configurations of time. Nor had the horse wranglers. The godlike men did understand that there would be little pleasure to this act. Some wondered if they should pay attention at all.

The cage imprisoning the bird disapperared. The bird

pulled himself forward and an eternal child giggled. He whimpered in response, and the whimper echoed throughout the auditorium. He puzzled over what he was supposed to do; no one had even tried to tell him. He looked toward the demon sitting a millimeter in the air. The gnawing inside was suddenly more powerful, but he ignored it as best he could; he wanted the demon to give him a clue. But the demon just fondled his penis. The crawling bird reached toward him; the demon appeared not to notice.

The bird crawled back and forth on the stage; he did not know what else to do. Splinters pierced his belly and blood dripped on the stage. Before the physical pain became too intense, the demon (or somebody) made the splinters disappear and the bird was whole. The blood on the stage did not disappear.

The bird could not bear the stares of the godlike men. The gnawing inside grew more fierce. He thought the faces were merging into one, and he saw the orange sun and yellow clouds.

And he heard the singing snakes. They whispered about him, laughed at him, cursed him; they were all disappointed in him. Something inside the bird told him that he was not seeing the snakes at all: only the godlike men. He could not accept that. He was being watched by evil beings who could not comprehend him. The golden singing snakes had always been that way; why should it be any different now?

Finally he gave up searching for pity and warmth where he knew there was none. He lay down in the center of the stage.

He sang. At first he sang so low the godlike men could barely hear him. He concentrated on lessening the gnawing inside rather than on his singing. He closed his eyes so he would not see the snakes looking at him. Then he sang louder so he could not hear them laughing at him. He hoped that if he sang loud and long enough, they would go away and never bother him again. Something inside told him it was doubtful, but to try nonetheless.

His song had neither rhythm nor construction, neither sophistication nor direction. He sang the notes he wanted, when he wanted. He expected the snakes to sing back at him, to drown out his song, but that did not happen. He did not care that they were silent; he cared for nothing.

The demon, the fat man, and the lawyer were quite pleased. The fat man jabbed the lawyer; then he jabbed the demon. The song was beautiful, considering that it was such a hideous wail. They told themselves that with this act, the race of godlike men would surely discover depression.

But the godlike men were not depressed. They were still confused. They listened to the bird's wail to give the bird (and the fat man) a chance. As the wail (for they did not think of it as a song) grew louder, they became angry. They felt they understood it; they were moved by it, but not in the way the demon and the lawyer had expected them to be. The wail surfaced emotions and concepts they had always possessed but had drowned in their gaiety and game-playing.

The wail was more powerful than the sirens' song. It did not select emotions, nor did it carefully probe souls. It shoveled into the godlike men and brought forth visions of loneliness, heartache, and the fear of dying. It made the godlike men feel useless and insignificant, for all their great powers and varied identities. The wail washed over them, and they forgot their glittering surroundings and petty ambitions; they forgot the praise they had lavished on the fat man; they were angered and disappointed. Soon some conjured cotton into their ears. Some talked to themselves and clenched their fists. Some wiped sweat off their foreheads and spat on the floor. The wail still washed over them, crept into them. Despite all their defenses, there was nothing but the wail.

The crawling bird forgot about the snakes watching him. He strained for more power and volume. For him there was nothing but the song and the gnawing inside.

After singing for an hour, the bird became exhausted and he wanted to look at the orange sun and yellow clouds. Gradually the song lessened in volume until there was silence. The bird opened his eyes and saw the godlike men staring at him. He wondered what had happened to the sun and clouds; then he realized he was still far from home. He wondered, briefly, if he had performed satisfactorily (for surely they had wanted him to sing). He felt anew the gnawing inside, at its most painful; he decided he did not care what the demon and his friends thought.

The fat man walked onstage. He beamed at the crowd.

He asked, "Well, did you learn something from the crawling bird?"

The Queen shrugged in royal displeasure. "We have elected to forget it," she said.

The portly author fired his elephant gun in the air. "Next time I won't miss," he said.

The superhero said, "That crawling bird is a menace. And I should know. Take him back where he came from."

An eternal child giggled and pointed at the superhero. "No wonder they call him the Big Red Cheese," he said to his godlike parents.

The insidious Oriental doctor toyed with an infernal machine and aimed it at the crawling bird. "I second the Big Red Cheese's motion," he said. "And dear fat man, if you do not agree, the crawling bird will die a thousand horrible deaths."

The poet, yearning for the return of blissful childhood, walked up to the fat man. "Fooey," he said. He thumbed his nose at the fat man and then walked away, stroking his wavy white hair.

"There are things we do not care to know," said the Queen. "We are not the only one who has forgotten them. And we might add that we have done something else. We have elected to confiscate all your fame and glory."

The race of godlike men cheered their approval, and the glorious, history-making fair was over.

6. The demon, the lawyer, and the fat man sat in the demon's apartment. The black curtains were drawn; several candles in green glass bowls resting on shelves and tables provided the trio with light. The fat man, sitting in the Morris chair, puffed his pipe and kept pulling his trouser cuffs over his white socks. The lawyer drank lemonade and chewed bubble gum. The demon sat in the air and cleaned his hands by licking them with his forked tongue. Everything was the same as before the fair, except they were depressed.

"So this is what depression is," said the lawyer. "I didn't know it would feel so horrible."

"It is all your fault, pig-lover," said the fat man, patting his great bulk. "If you had not talked me into this, then I would still have all my fame and glory. Do you realize that even my wife is ignoring me? Do you realize that?"

"I'm too depressed to care," said the demon.

"It's not our fault!" said the lawyer, spilling his lemonade on the black leather sofa. "It's yours, you fat has-been! If you'd handled it right, then the *people* would have been depressed and not *us*!"

The fat man scowled. "You had better not let my gunsel hear you talk that way. At least he still likes me despite your big ideas and my ill-fortune. Humph!" He rubbed one of his chins. "Instead of being on the top where I belong, I am at the bottom. Right with you two."

"It's still your fault," said the lawyer, sending the lemonade on the sofa to the anti-matter universe.

The demon snorted. "I imagine there's only one thing we can do."

"And just what is that?" asked the fat man, not really caring what the answer was.

The demon pointed at the ceiling. "Do it again."

The lawyer gaped at the demon. "What in the name of sin are you talking about?"

The demon said, "We now know what depression is like, don't we? Aren't we trying to think of something to get us back on top? Aren't we open to new ideas and emotions? We most certainly are desperate characters. We succeeded, but in a way we didn't expect: we succeeded upon ourselves rather than upon the people. And we've proved, using ourselves as the test subjects, that the race of godlike man is, for the most part, human. All we have to do is to bring it out in others so they have to admit it."

The lawyer blew a bubble which burst. "Why, I think I know what you mean! It's just occurred to me: I now possess new and different insights: into myself, into godlike mankind, into the position of life in the universe. I think we can do it." He wiped the gum from his face.

The fat man uncrossed and crossed his ankles. "Friend demon, you have re-earned my respect. In fact, you are a genius! I will do it!"

"It might take a long time," said the demon. "And we'll have to think of something more imaginative than a mere crawling bird. I think we'll fail several times. But we'll do it. We'll really do it."

The fat man said, "Amazing. I no longer deplore eagerness. I am actually eager to begin." He conjured a glass of lemonade and gave it to the lawyer who accepted it with a grateful smile. "With whom shall we begin? The portly author? Shall we break his elephant gun? Or with the superhero? The Queen? The poet? Or shall we begin with the people at all? Perhaps somewhere else. . . ."

7. The crawling bird grabbed a sapling and pulled himself toward it. Already his belly was matted with scabs; he was sorry the demon's magic could not be with him forever. Already he was forgetting the events of the recent past; there was enough in his home world that he could not understand without puzzling over more. Seeing the orange-sun and the yellow clouds again did not fill him with the pleasure he had expected; he was still filled with remorse and the gnawing inside. Nothing was changed.

He heard the golden singing snakes, deep in the thickest areas of the jungle. He could imagine them wrapped about the red crooked limbs, hissing and thinking they were superior to every animal in the universe. The bird whimpered; he felt sorry for them, and he could not understand why. Maybe he had been changed, somehow and someway, after all.

The crawling bird wanted to sing to someone. Not to the snakes or to the godlike men; they would hate him for it. To his mate in the caves. She would know how he had been changed and she would return his song with hers. Maybe, somehow, she had been changed too. Maybe she felt less pain than he did.

Ignoring the rocks jabbing his belly, the crawling bird pulled himself toward the caves.

SLICES OF LIFE: ONE

The ace reporter woke instantly, rolled out of her circular bed heaped high with leopard furs, and exercised naked in front of her mirror; she admired her lean body, her turned-up nose, her brown eyes, and her black hair. Although godlike women usually remained in the background, preferring godlike men be the center of attention, the ace reporter was different. She wanted to be dynamic; she was; her personality was forceful, direct, charismatic. She wanted to rush out there and get that story; she did; she had written an article on the fat man's fair three days before it had been opened to the public. She wanted to be smarter than everybody else; she was; she could speculate upon the ethical structure of the universe for hours without repeating herself once. She wanted to be the sexiest godlike woman in the newspaper office; she was; that was a particulary difficult task since all godlike women were beautiful. However, the ace reporter was athletic, slender, almost boyish, and the godlike men attracted to her were mesmerized, simply because she *was* different. The ace reporter was quite correctly proud of herself.

Yet every morning, after concluding her exercises and sitting at her dresser fixing her hair (she could have fixed her hair mentally, but then it would have lacked that natural look), she wondered if she was *too* proud of herself. She had not found a godlike man worthy of her. She had always been alone, searching for someone more super than the rest. Once she considered having an affair with the Big Red Cheese, the most noted lover of her race. But she had decided he was silly.

Her apartment was spacious, with light green walls, white furniture, abstract paintings, twenty-five electrical outlets and two lamps plugged into each one, and a freezer full of frozen dinners which she heated instantly rather than waiting for them to heat in the oven; she was always too busy and too hungry to waste time with primitive customs. A big story could break at any moment; a big story could never wait for a frozen dinner, though it could wait while she fixed her hair.

The ace reporter brushed her teeth, sent trash to the anti-matter universe, and dressed herself in a green blouse, a white skirt, and green high-heeled shoes. She sharpened her pencils, drew a brand new notebook from a desk drawer, put a new tape in her recorder, and tossed them all in her leather saddlebag. She had to interview the romantic poet sometime before he drowned himself in the sea, so she could tell her readers of the ecstasy he felt every time he was reborn, so she could make her readers sympathize for his grieving widow and feel her joy when her husband's corpse came to life. But she had to go to the newspaper office first; perhaps something important had unexpectedly developed.

As she teleported herself to the office, the ace reporter wondered if she had done an interview with the romantic poet before. She had done interviews for eons. She was destined to begin repeating herself soon, if she had not already begun to do so. There was a limited number of godlike men to interview; the routine of life was rarely broken. The race of godlike men enjoyed reading interviews in the daily newspaper, but she did not know if the people liked news. There was rarely news.

She materialized beside the editor's desk in his private office. She heard the pounding of typewriters outside. Old newspapers and wadded paper littered the floor. The trash can was in a corner, and most of the wadded paper lay around it; the editor's aim was extremely poor. The editor had brown hair streaked with white; he had dull eyes, and a dimpled chin. As usual, he wore a battered fedora, a brown suit with a loosened brown tie, and an unbuttoned white shirt with thin blue vertical lines in it. He puffed a huge cigar. (The ace reporter knew a green eyeshade and elastic sleeve garters lay waiting in the editor's bottom left-hand drawer——waiting for the cries of, "Remake the front page! We're getting out an extra!" They had never been worn.)

"Good morning, Chief."

The editor looked up from copy and puffed smoke into the ace reporter's face. "How many times do I have to tell you: don't call me Chief!"

"Sorry, Chief. Listen: have any stories broken!"

"Of course not! Stories never break any more. Go out there and get me that interview with the romantic poet. And go out there and get me a story! Don't come back unless you *have* a story! *Make* a story if you have to! Understand?"

"Sure, Chief."

"And don't call—aw, forget it. Just go."

"Right away, Chief."

And the ace reporter went to the beach.

She asked the romantic poet many penetrating questions, each designed to cut to the very core of his existence. The ace reporter hoped that her questions would confound him, or at least make him hesitate. The romantic poet answered them immediately, as if he were reciting a poem he had written, a poem that bored him. Finally, the ace reporter realized she had indeed interviewed the romantic poet before—not once, but twice. She concluded the session quickly and slowly walked away while he drowned himself. She did not need to stay or to talk with his wife. She could go home and write the story from her files, combining the two previous stories to write something fresh. She did not have to go out there and make a story because her editor told her to do that every day; she always returned to the office empty-handed and he did not seem to care; in fact, he seemed to expect it.

The cool breeze disarrayed the ace reporter's hair. She teleported her shoes to her apartment and felt the wet sand squish between her toes and the water wash over her feet. She pretended she was completely alone, that there was not another godlike man alive. When that ploy failed to cheer her, she tried to think of a story, of ways to make some news. She knew in advance she would think of nothing, but still she concentrated on the problem.

The zany imp from the fifth dimension materalized beside her. He wore a purple uniform with yellow boots and a tiny round purple hat. He was small and skinny; he looked fragile enough to shatter should he accidently collide with a flying squirrel. His smile stretched across his face; his red eyes glowed with mischievous passion; his nose was long and slender, phallic in an antic way.

The ace reporter hated the zany imp from the fifth dimension; once she likened his nose to a stuffed worm. It was an unfortunate situation, because the zany imp was in love with her. Since he had discovered his love, he had gradually lost his zaniness and was now as boring as everyone else.

"Go away, toadsucker," the ace reporter said.

The zany imp landed and knelt beside her. The water slapped his breeches. "Listen, sweetie, I'll make a deal. There're all kinds of stories in the fifth dimension; all you have to do to get them is make the right contacts; and let me tell you, sweetie, I got 'em! All you have to do is love me and you'll be the greatest reporter this world has ever seen. What do you say, sweetie? Is it a deal?"

"I'm already the greatest reporter this world has ever seen," she said, walking past him. "And I've been to the fifth dimension. What a dull place!"

"Oh." The zany imp from the fifth dimension said his name backwards and disappeared in a puff of smoke. As he faded away, he said, "I'll be back in ninety days, sweetie, with another deal! It'll be the greatest deal of all! You'll see! You'll see! It'll be an offer you can't refuse! You'll love me yet!"

Once again alone on the beach, the ace reporter forgot about the visit by the zany imp. There was nothing worth remembering. She continued her walk until she decided it was time to go to the office and write the story.

The chief thought it was a magnificent piece of writing. But what the hell did he know?

CHAPTER TWO

1. But the demon, the lawyer, and the fat man had not reckoned with the vehemence of godlike hatred.

Seven days after the Queen had elected to confiscate all their fame and glory, the populace sighted them taking an early morning stroll. The lawyer wore his finest black silk suit with his most beautiful plastic red flower in the lapel. His shoes tapped with every step. The gold handle of his sword-cane intermittently twinkled with reflected sunlight. The fat man, dressed in his most immaculate white suit, lumbered along next to the lawyer; he mumbled something about the marvelous joys of exercise. The huge demon floated behind them. He fondled his penis, which dangled below his folded legs, and he trimmed his long red fingernails by nipping at them delicately with his beak.

Suddenly people yelled at them. They were called such foul names as washout, has-been, and dud. The fat man was called a shadow; the demon, an angel; and the lawyer, a pig. At first they stared in silence at the people leaning from windows and shaking their fists, at the skywriter painting insults in the sky, and at eternal children making an universally obscene gesture. They had hoped to hatch new schemes without disturbance, but when that hope was dashed, they desired to finish their walk with a dignity befitting their lofty goals, no matter how difficult that would be.

The lawyer twirled his sword-cane and fingered his plastic flower. "Friend fat man," he said, "I've just noticed something."

"And what might that be?" asked the fat man.

"Your gunsel's no longer sulking behind us. Not once during the past hour have I glimpsed him ducking into an alleyway. Did he decide to stay home today?"

The demon, wincing at a particulary explicit insult concerning the size of his penis, said, "Perhaps we should have noticed his wisdom sooner." A freak air current upset him, and he almost toppled into the fat man before righting himself.

The fat man rubbed his nose and brushed dust from his white coat sleeve. "My gunsel is afraid and hiding in the basement of my home."

"Why in the basement?" asked the lawyer. "Doesn't he have a private bathroom?"

"I am sorry you brought that up," said the fat man. "My wife, who made life unbearable for me several days ago, is now in the process of doing the same to my gunsel. She is remodeling his bathroom. She wants it to be an art gallery."

"Full of bright, optimistic paintings?" asked the demon.

"Indeed," replied the fat man.

The lawyer suddenly ceased to look dapper and confident. He pressed the button on his sword-cane and pricked the tip of his finger on the blade. He watched a drop of blood fall into a golden gutter. "Now *that*," he said, "is a painting."

His friends chose to ignore his statement, and they walked in silence for a while longer, ignoring the jeers and catcalls of everyone who saw them.

It was an extremely lovely morning on Earth. The bees did not buzz too loud as they searched in vain for flowers among the huge apartment complexes, nor did the dogs bark at the three friends. Had it not been for the extenuating circumstances, they would have thought of a hundred brilliant ideas, each one assured of success (or so they would have thought). But nothing came to them; they walked as if the white, fluffy clouds were deep and black and pregnant with rain. Their one consolation was that they were not completely depressed; they still had hope.

As they neared the demon's apartment, the lawyer said, "Friend fat man, something else has occurred to me."

"Then out with it, man! Today I have no patience with indirect statements."

"Well, if your wife is making life unbearable for you and your gunsel, then you must not want to stay at your home."

The fat man knelt to pull up his white socks. "I am gratified you brought up that subject. She has stolen my key to the front door and I do not wish to break in every time I want to sleep or have a drink of gin. I was hoping that, if you and the demon have no objections, my gunsel might stay with you and I might stay with the demon." He paused, licking his lips. "At least until your landladies lease your respective apartments to someone else, since they too must hate you."

"I have no objections," said the demon. "The lawyer and I made a deal with our landladies: they wouldn't kick us out if we took out the garbage so the garbageman could send it to the anti-matter universe."

"I, likewise, have no objections," said the dapper lawyer. "That is, if the gunsel knows how to keep his place."

"I assure you," said the fat man, "you will not even know that he is there."

A few days later the race of godlike men began to play practical jokes on the trio. Every morning for a week the demon had to cast a spell to repair his blue-tinged picture windows and to send the unwanted rocks to another portion of the planet. Someone stole his paintings of Hell; it took him some time to recover them. Someone clogged up his commode. The fat man lost all his white suits, and he was not ready for a change of image. He searched all over Earth for replacements, but every tailor (when he could convince them to talk to him) assured him that there had never been such a thing as a white suit. Eventually the fat man was forced to spend precious energy creating white suits out of nothingness. No one knew what had happened to the gunsel, if anything had happened at all. The demon suspected that a thin man pretending to push up loose false teeth with his thumb had molested the gunsel in an unseemly fashion, but he could not be sure. The demon and the fat man bore their misfortunes as stoically as possible; they were convinced that they were in the right and that nothing could stop them from achieving their goal; a little sacrifice was called for.

The lawyer was another matter. One morning he woke to find one hundred and twenty-six pigs in his apartment. The fact that they were all immaculate did not placate him. Seven of the foul, pink creatures were in his bathtub. The lawyer was so distressed that he could not get rid of them himself, and the demon had to do the job for him. Afterward the demon and the fat man tried to calm him, but he paced back and forth, screaming at the top of his grating nasal voice.

"It wouldn't be so bad," he said, "if Kitty weren't ignoring me! Last night I stole into her bedroom and poured thousand island salad dressing—her favorite—into her sleeve. Even when it reached her armpit and dripped onto her bosom, she didn't glance at me. She eyed the Big Red Cheese and whispered sweet nothings in his cauliflower ears!"

"It's just as well," said the demon.

"I agree," said the fat man. "She was never any good for you."

"But what's the use in being alive if you can't mingle with people no good for you?" asked the lawyer, rolling up his sleeves, preparing to scrub the walls and the floor.

The demon and the fat man said nothing. The answer, if voiced, would have depressed them too much.

Soon the race of godlike men tired of practical jokes, and the three friends were subjected to the worse punishment of all. They were forgotten. No one spoke to them; no one hated them; no one pitied them. When the lawyer walked down the street, unseeing people bumped into him. When he said, "Excuse me," people did not seem to hear. The demon could not give away paintings he had tired of because no one would look at them. Even the gunsel suffered; he could find no one who would become nervous when he shadowed people on dark and lonely streets. It was a sorry fate indeed.

Only the fat man bore his burden with good humor. He sat all day in the demon's Morris chair. He read books, took off his white shoes and told the gunsel to shine them until the scuff marks did not show, and chuckled to himself. He seemed pleased about something, but the demon and the lawyer could not understand what. One day they discussed the fat man's attitude as they walked through the farms at the North Pole, tended by the pigs in trenchcoats.

The glaring sun beat upon them; they used their powers to cool themselves. The fields had tall, healthy green grass which bowed under the pressure of a brisk breeze. In the distance were the corn and tomato fields, fields that stretched unbroken for kilometers. Occasionally they saw a pig driving a tractor, or two pigs of opposite sexes running hand-in-hand through the grass, searching for a place where they could be alone. The demon and the lawyer understood that wish; they needed to be alone, too, but for different reasons; they needed to sort out their lives so they could return to the business of altering destiny.

"I can't understand the fat man's attitude," said the lawyer, playing with his ruffled sleeves. "It doesn't make any sense. He's lost more fame and glory then the two of us combined, and it doesn't affect him in the least. He just sits there, reading and smoking that pipe smelling like dishwater."

"His pipe smells not only like dishwater, but like grease or stale bread. He changes the odor whenever he tires of it. Believe me, I know; I have to live with it." The demon ran his hand across his four white nipples and practiced breathing fire, a new trait he wished to add to his idenity.

"But why doesn't he care? At first I thought I could live without fame and glory, but I've found I can't. We must succeed so we can bask in all the fame and glory we desire, otherwise this depression I feel will drive me mad. And he does nothing! We don't even know what he's chuckling at!"

The demon drifted to the ground and stabbed a tomato with his beak. He pulled the tomato from his beak and bit it. The red juices ran down his hand. He stared at the lawyer. "It must be something quite humorous. It has to be, if his mental state is as low as ours."

A thought occurred to the lawyer. "Did you ever think to ask him?"

"No. Did You?"

"No."

"Then I have a suggestion," said the demon. "We should pool our courage and resolve—what little we have during these dreary days—and ask him together."

"A brilliant solution," said the lawyer.

And they went to the demon's apartment and asked the fat man, who sat with a new edition of *The Big Red*

45

Cheese's Existential Philosophy resting on his huge lap; and he listened to them intently. Finally, "This is most ironic," said the fat man. "You two are beset by serious doubts about the righteousness of our cause, and yet you are the very ones who convinced me to continue when I was ready to give up. You two are both characters, I assure you, if you do not mind my saying so."

"We don't mind," said the demon, catching a fly with his forked tongue. "But we wish you would tell us what you're chuckling at. The deep rumbles in your stomach are disturbing."

"Did it ever occur to you that our punishment is a blessing in disguise?"

"I don't understand," said the lawyer.

"Neither do I," said the demon, breathing fire and accidently singeing his favorite painting of Hell. He decided that breathing fire might be an inconvenient addition to his identity.

"Then I shall explain."

The fat man raised a finger to the ceiling, then pressed it against his flabby cheek. "Once all eyes were upon us; people wondered what we were going to do next. Now people do not care what we do, as they do not care for our goals; they no longer watch us. Therefore, we have all the privacy in the universe. We can be as diabolical, as cruel, and as crafty as we want; we no longer have to worry if our schemes are socially acceptable; we are in control. Think of it, my friends. And here you are, yearning for the return of the old days you detested with such fervor." He paused and smiled. "I believe that explains everything."

"It doesn't explain everything," said the demon.

"It doesn't?" asked the lawyer.

"What were you chuckling at?" asked the demon.

"At you two," said the fat man. "I thought it amusing that you had not grasped the facts. But enough of that. A plan has recently occurred to me and the time has come to discuss it." He conjured a glass of lemonade into the lawyer's hand.

"Why, thank you," said the lawyer.

2. The eternal child stood on the golden roof of a golden apartment building and cursed at the flying figure silhouetted against the blue sky (the figure of the lonely hawkman, wearing wings and an orange mask and red tights, the curator of the museum of the past). It was so hard for his retarded mind to think of new sentences; he had been cursing for so long. And it was so hard to scream; his tongue did not want to move and his throat hurt; the only times he had ever spoken were when he cursed. And his neck hurt from the strain of looking straight up; his eyes hurt from the blinding yellow sun. To rest his neck, he looked down and spat on the golden roof. Then he looked again to the sky and once more cursed. Soon the lonely hawkman was out of sight, but the eternal child continued cursing. He listened to his rasping words and held his fists so tight that his dirty fingernails made raw half-moons in his palms. He stamped his foot again and pain shot up his knee. He did not want to cry, but tears fell down his cheeks. He screamed one final, long curse and prayed that the hawkman would hear, be insulted, and return; the sky remained empty. Soon a flying squirrel flew overhead. The eternal child knelt and beat his tiny fists on the golden roof until his knuckles bled; he had been ignored again.

The eternal child had a round, freckled face and large green eyes, brown hair and a pug nose, thin arms and a high-pitched voice. He wore baggy trousers and a white t-shirt. His shoes had holes and one had lost its heel. His parents belonged to the race of godlike men and his friends were also eternal children. Yet he thought of himself as the eternal child, as if there were no others. He lived in colorful dreams, usually for the moment, without growth or change. He was not flesh and blood, but a synthetic thing, an important afterthought to the society of the Earth. If he had known, he would not have cared, for he did not have the intellect to comprehend the subtle difference.

Despite the loving presence of his parents and the casual comradeship of his friends, he was alone. His parents loved him because he had been created to be the recipient of their love; the other eternal children were almost exactly like him, and that was their only bond. He was unlike the others in that he spoke only to curse and he possessed crude qualities of perception. He realized that he was ugly and mediocre when compared to the godlike men. He wanted to wear a red costume and fly like the Big Red Cheese, or build statues of falling dogs like the solitary man with the red beard, or salute with two right arms and pour garbage into the sun like the galactic hero, or spend his time doing all the work and getting none of the credit like a certain diplomat. Whenever he realized that he was going to live forever, he suddenly became tired of the fleeting instances of safety and comfort his parents gave him, grew tired of sleeping alone in dark rooms, became tired of the emptiness and pain in his heart, grew tired of mindlessly hating female eternal children.

Resting on the golden roof, he picked up golden gravel and spread his fingers, counting each rock as it fell. He wished that the hawkman would fly over him again; he wanted to curse more. He shook his hair into his eyes so he would not have to see the world all at once. His pain and frustration welled up inside him, and his hands shook. He bit his lower lip and closed his eyes. Perhaps darkness would help. Darkness: blackness.

Blackness. That was what he always saw in his parents' apartment. He knew that he should go home. There, safe between the close walls of his room, his parents' soft voices filtering through the wood, he would not feel the overwhelming need to curse. His mind would be free to dart from dream to dream, from desire to desire, and the specter of reality would be blotted out. Trying not to shake nervously with each step, the eternal child walked home. He watched his feet, and he did not notice the salutations of his comrades.

At home, he sat down on a light red rug in the middle of the living room floor and played cards. He believed that if he concentrated hard enough on the cards, then all his other thoughts would disappear. He had used this tactic before; it had never worked; this time was no exception. Only one lamp was on. As night fell, he paid no attention to the darkness; he could barely see his cards. His eyelids were heavy, and he wanted to sleep.

His parents returned. His father, the romantic poet, drowned himself in the sea at least once a day. His mother was the romantic poet's wife who wrote novels and understood that all godlike men, forever struggling between good and evil, must ultimately face their own creations, gothically speaking. The eternal child glanced at them and returned to his cards.

His parents could do many things he could not. They could create matter out of nothingness, change their appearances at will, and understand dirty jokes. They were the biggest of all to his tiny eyes; they were taller than the tallest buildings, longer than the longest streets, larger than the largest parents of other children. His mother snapped her fingers and another light turned on; it was still difficult for the eternal child to see. They stood over him and watched him play; they said he was cuter than all the other eternal children (who looked so much like him). They lifted him and held him to their chests, pressing him between them, and it was good that they loved him, because the floor was so far away. He was always frightened when they held him, but he looked forward to the experience; the more fear he showed, the more they loved him.

The next morning, as he kicked off his blankets, he felt his atoms break up. His atoms swirled around and around, creating a tiny wind inside his room. They flew out the window, into the misty morning of Earth, and sped across the planet.

3. The eternal child faced the demon, the lawyer, and the fat man. He felt a touch of hope; for the first time godlike men were paying attention to him. Yet he could not remember who these three were; they seemed vaguely familiar. He decided that it made no difference. He greeted them the only way he knew how: by cursing. He used his best curses, voicing them with all the sincerity he could muster. Reveling in the sheer joy and release of cursing, he strained his throat and danced up and down in hatred. For once there were godlike men who would listen, who would allow him to hold nothing back. He felt total harmony between himself and his emotions. Perhaps after this he would no longer need his parents to lift him from the floor and love him; all the comfort he needed would come from himself alone, and he would never be disappointed again. His face turned red with effort as he closed his eyes and listened to the poetry of his curses. He cursed for twenty minutes, until a jet of air from the demon's four nostrils sent him crashing against a wall.

"He's certainly loud," said the lawyer, shoving the tip of his sword into the eternal child's face.

The fat man lumbered to the pair and pushed away the sword with his finger. "And incomprehensible." he smiled at the lawyer. "But he is a guest, and he should be treated as one."

"Awww," said the lawyer, walking to a yellow easy chair by the picture window. "I want to frighten him. He reminds me of a pig." When he sat down, he was bathed in blue sunlight.

"We'll gain nothing from it," said the demon, massaging his sore nostrils.

"Please?"

"You may not frighten him," said the fat man, "but you may sit in the Morris chair. I have sat in it for so long that my buttocks are becoming meaty and rounded, incapable of bouncing with my every movement and of rolling into a comfortable position when I shift my weight. The skin is red and tacky; the blood will not flow through them. My buttocks have been asleep for five days, and I am afraid that I have not noticed that fact until this very instant. So please sit in the Morris chair. It is your favorite, I believe."

The lawyer smiled and pushed a button; the blade slipped inside his cane. He stood up and walked toward the chair, pulling down his black jacket so the wrinkles would not show. He sat down, crossing his legs, parodying the fat man's manner. The demon conjured a glass of lemonade for him.

The eternal child shrank against the statue of Behemoth. From the corner of his eye he saw a red bloodstain on the silver wall where his head had struck; but when he felt his head, there was no wound. The fat man stood over him, but he could not see the godlike man's expression for the vast bulk of his stomach. The eternal child saw how white the fat man's clothes were; he yearned for the safe blackness of his parents' apartment. His life had changed, and now he wanted it to be as it had been before. The fat man ruffled the eternal child's hair, and the eternal child shrank from the clammy touch.

"You are going to remain silent?" asked the fat man. "Of course you are." He walked away from the eternal child and did deep kneebends to awaken his buttocks.

"Where's your gunsel?" asked the demon. "He's suffered as much as we. He should be here to see the object of his salvation."

"He knows and he has seen," said the fat man, breathing heavily. "But do not ask me how. There are some mysteries of the infinite universe that not even godlike men may question."

"I suppose you're correct," said the demon, turning his head one hundred and eighty degrees to inspect the eternal child. "However, it pains me to admit it."

The eternal child shivered. He rubbed his arms, hoping to spread warmth through his body.

The lawyer held his empty glass toward the eternal child. "My friend, it's been said many times before: those who are cold should not expect sympathy from the warm."

"As we should know," said the demon.

The fat man took a white silk handkerchief from his vest pocket and wiped the sweat from his forehead. He sat down on a high-backed chair with gargoyles at the top. He lit his pipe. The smoke smelled like decaying fish. "Enough of this frivolity," he said. "It is time to get down to some serious business."

"I agree," said the lawyer, tapping his fingers on the sword-cane. "Then perhaps tonight I can persuade Kitty to stop ignoring me."

"And since all my business is extremely serious," said the demon, floating next to the eternal child and looking down at him, "we have no more obstacles before us."

The fat man puffed at his pipe and nodded in satisfaction. "Then I shall explain why we need a specimen of the android race we choose to call the eternal children. The race itself is among the most important particulars of our world, yet it is the most ignored. Why should a world of immortal godlike men have need of a retarded, dirty race of brats who never grow and who never change? There is one very good reason."

"Must you be so long-winded?" asked the lawyer. "Your circular reasoning is becoming progressively more sterile."

The fat man snapped his fingers and pointed at the lawyer. "My indignant friend, you have hit upon it!"

"I have?"

The eternal child squirmed. He hoped that his parents would unexpectedly pass by the apartment, sense that their child was in danger, and rescue him. He vividly imagined them tearing down the walls and shattering the blue-tinged glass and lifting him safely into their loving arms. But he knew that would not happen. His father was probably preparing to drown again, and afterward his mother would cram thirty years' worth of grief and white washing into one hour.

The demon laughed deeply. "Of course! There're only three generations of godlike mankind. But raising brats had been a habit for so long that it was one of the few things godlike men couldn't sacrifice for immortality!"

The lawyer looked puzzled. He pursed his thin lips and rolled his eyes in uncomprehending frustration. "But why did people create a race of children that remind me of pigs?"

The fat man shrugged. "Things did not work out for the best."

The demon rubbed his hands in glee. "Ah, friend fat man, your mind is ecstatically satanic!"

The fat man acknowledged the glowing compliment with a humbling wave of his hand. "Although your statement is undoubtedly sincere, I do not believe that even you, friend demon, have grasped exactly what use I plan to make of this eternal child."

"Tell us!" demanded the lawyer, bouncing up and down in the Morris chair. "We must know!"

The fat man stood and did deep kneebends. "Instead of trying to bring depression to everyone at once, we should work on a few godlike men at a time. The parents of eternal children live their lives at a breakneck speed like any other decent couple, doing the same thing over and over again as rapidly as possible, but they need something constant. If we should remove that constant factor from a couple here, and then a couple there, and so on and so on—well, I leave the rest to your fertile imaginations."

"I don't get it," said the lawyer.

The demon grinned. His beak was an interesting study in contortion. "What if an eternal child should change?"

"Huh?" asked the lawyer.

The fat man patted his gut and sat down. "What if one should grow as did the children of mere man? What if one should mature?"

The eternal child rubbed his eyes. He rubbed them until they were red and wondered why they did not stop itching. Then the back of his head itched, and his stomach hurt. He had been shaking for five minutes. He was angry at these godlike men; he wanted to curse them. As he finally succumbed to his desire—though he knew it would bring him more pain—the demon cast a spell over him and he fell asleep. It was not a peaceful sleep.

"Such an ugly child," the demon mumbled.

"Fat man, what you suggest is impossible!" said the lawyer.

"You still have doubts," said the fat man. "That is good, very good, for that means you will examine every aspect of my brilliant plan. Believe me, lawyer, the maturity of an eternal child will be such an unexpected factor in the lives of the parents who love him that it will bring about hopelessness and depression without fail."

"Your plan is folly. Pure folly," said the lawyer.

"So's messing around with Kitty," said the demon, "but that's never deterred *you*."

"That has nothing to do with it!"

The fat man chuckled; his stomach rippled seismically until he stopped. "I did not say *we* would change him. At this very moment my gunsel is threatening the shrink."

Sudden, uncontrollable fear swallowed the lawyer as he savored the implications of the fat man's words. He caressed his sword-cane. The shrink. Hhe realized that if anyone could do the impossible, it was the shrink, one of the most mysterious godlike men of all.

4. Normally the shrink, a student of ignored passions and idiosyncrasies of godlike mankind, well-known for his hatred of anything that smacked of mere man, did not do what others wished of him. However, walking his favorite dark golden alleyway and watching the silver rays of the moon play over golden buildings, he was shadowed by the gunsel. Normally, he felt superior during his walks; few disturbed him. Normally, he was free to pursue any dark thought he desired, and he could contemplate any glorious idiosyncrasy of godlike mankind. But like all others, he did not think that the gunsel still had the nerve to shadow someone. When he heard the carefully calculated sound of footsteps behind him and turned to determine who would dare interrupt his brooding, he saw no one; the gunsel had disappeared among the shadows and now leaned against golden walls . . . watching. The shrink felt godlike terror. Although he fancied himself the master of the unknown paths of godlike minds, he was afraid of facing the unknown in a physical form; immeasurable godlike terror was something new to him.

Returning to his golden stone castle atop an eternally stormy mountain, he calmed down enough to wonder who had shadowed him. He sat in the library and toyed with the dials of a machine that projected thoughts on a screen. Because he was reluctant to admit his terror, he told himself that he had simply been filled with disquiet. Although he knew godlike men did nothing without a purpose, he could not think of who had anything to gain by frightening someone as powerful as he.

The shrink was the epitome of plastic godlike mankind. He did not realize that of all the different identities in use, only his seemed to be an unnatural charade; there was no sincerity in his heart. Unconcerned with his appearance, he wore a light blue shirt, a red tie, and loafers because he thought that was what shrinks should wear. His face was round and puffy; his black hair was thin; his mustache needed trimming. Whenever he spoke to someone, he smiled. After he turned away and no one could see his face, his mouth resumed the tight, grim expression that suited his disposition more aptly. He was a cold machine, colder than the dials over which his hands now roamed; he was forever prepared to discover some hidden facet of the godlike mind. Suddenly his games, his knowledge, and his powers were no longer a source of comfort and joy to him. He was as frail as any god. His voice quivering, he said, "All right! I know you're there! Come out, come out, wherever you are!"

He received no reply. The shrink stared into the night and imagined it creeping upon him. He said, "Please?"

The fat man, the demon, and the lawyer entered the library. The fat man said, "See? I told you he would be receptive."

The demon nodded. "And as usual, you were correct."

The dapper young lawyer frowned. Pointing his sword-cane at the shrink, he said, "He has the nose of a pig. And look at him shake. Do you really think we can trust a godlike man like that?" Although his tone revealed no trace of nervousness, the lawyer did not glance at the shrink. He fully expected their victim to cloud their minds and send them to the brink of madness.

The demon had no such worries. He gave the lawyer a light slap on the shoulder and said, "Your concern is misplaced; trust has nothing to do with it."

"Fear does," said the fat man. "Now take a look, friend lawyer. He wants to ignore me, but he is nevertheless afraid of me. Even without my former reputation, I am still a force to be reckoned with." Seeing a wave of jealousy pass over the lawyer's face, the fat man added. "And you are no slouch, either."

Under the circumstances the lawyer had to consider that one of the most genuine left-handed compliments he had ever been given. He politely thanked the fat man.

The demon floated to the shrink and asked, "Do you want to ignore me, too?"

The shrink tugged at his red tie. "Yes."

"Have you forgotten that five hundred years ago you denounced me in a speech to the assembled race?"

"Yes."

"You'll be happy to know that I've forgotten the incident, too. You're so far beneath my notice that were it not for the pressures of time and the lawyer, I would have constructed the proper machines myself." The demon waved his hands, and the sleeping eternal child, lying stiff and straight, floated into the room. "Make him mature," the demon commanded.

"Right now," said the lawyer, his voice an octave higher than usual.

"Please do not delay," said the fat man. "I have no patience with useless and futile delays."

"But I can't do that," said the shrink, mustering his courage. "Nobody can do that. It's unheard of."

The fat man smiled and chuckled. "My dear sir, you are not quite a character, if you do not mind my saying so. And I am sure you do not mind, because you have no choice in the matter. You can make the eternal child mature because we want you to."

"In a world where anything can happen," said the lawyer, "rest assured, it will."

"It won't take twenty minutes," said the demon, turning his head three hundred and sixty degrees to inspect the library. Usually he turned his head silently, but this time he made his vertebrae crack loudly to further terrify the shrink. It was a cheap, theatrical trick, but it served its purpose; the shrink paled slightly. "Then you'll be free to convince all others of your meaningless powers," the demon continued. "Think of it, shrink. To be able to rebuild your pitiful confidence. Doesn't it sound peachy to you?"

"And we'll leave you alone," said the lawyer.

"He is not being quite receptive enough," said the fat man. "I shall have to call in my gunsel."

"No! No! I'll do it! I'll do it in less than twenty minutes! He'll be more mature than any of us!"

"You don't have to go that far," said the lawyer.

"He only has to go as far as his basement," said the fat man. "My gunsel told me his most impressive equipment is there."

"I hope it's more impressive than his library," said the demon. "I memorized these books eons ago." He held up the shrink's appointment book. "And he's spending all day tomorrow psychoanalyzing the Big Red Cheese. How pedestrian!" He pointed his finger and the eternal child floated to his side.

The lawyer grabbed the shrink by the scuff of his neck and pulled him to a standing position. He attempted to drag him in the proper direction, but he lacked enough pure physical strength. With a gesture, the fat man stopped the lawyer from trying again. The lawyer pursed his lips, considered the matter, let go of the shrink, then bowed and said, "After you, shrink."

The shrink stared at the lawyer.

"Don't think of revenge," said the lawyer nervously. "The gunsel's my guest."

"Not forever," replied the shrink.

"Cease this violent nonsense!" said the fat man. "Shrink, one day you will thank us for your humiliation. We would convince you of the righteousness of our cause, but to attempt to do so while you are in this inexplicable foul mood would be folly." He chuckled. "Merely take us to your basement."

The shrink shrugged and walked out of the room. He considered pushing the self-destruct button beside the door jamb before the others could follow him out of the room—at worst it would have shaken them up and he would have had time to plan his next move—but as he made up his mind, the demon sighted the mechanism and sent it up to the anti-matter universe.

"Meddler," the shrink mumbled.

Even the satanic demon was impressed by the shrink's basement; it took him fully ten minutes to realize the purpose of the first machine he studied. The doorway to the basement was actually the doorway to the thirty-second dimension, a universe so fearsome and mysterious that godlike mankind had studied little of it. The golden stone walls protecting the shrink's equipment from the ravages of the thirty-second dimension were lined with books and machines. Dusty tables, file cabinets, and tinier machines were cluttered about, and the pathways were barely large enough for the fat man to squeeze himself through. The demon was thankful that he floated above the litter, for his bulk was greater than the fat man's.

The lawyer detested the dank air; he changed it and sniffed fresh air briefly. Then the shrink changed the air back to irritate him. The lawyer looked to the demon and the fat man to see if they would support him if he argued with the shrink, but they were too enthralled inspecting notes and machines to care about anything as trivial as air.

Gliding about in an attempt to show the shrink that he also did not care much about the odor of air, the lawyer walked to a thick window and stared at the thirty-second dimension. His eyes grew wide and his sword-cane clattered on the tile floor. He saw vast, unending blackness, blinking red and blue lights, billowing purple clouds, and thin orange roads leading to the stars. The roads intersected with one another, bent with the wind, and were held up by nothing. Huge chunks of land floated about in the vastness like kites lost by eternal children. The lawyer wanted to turn away; the indescribable magnificence of the view made him feel too small, too worthless; it was as if he had suddenly realized that all his hopes and dreams, even his lust for Kitty, were immaterial when he stared at the true glories of the unrelenting universe. He found it difficult to believe that with the return of depression godlike mankind would be fired again with the desire to conquer infinite territory. Yet he held on firmly to his belief. It was the only thing that could save his sanity during these troubled times.

The lawyer finally bent over to pick up his sword-cane and saw the shrink smirking. "What's the matter with you?"

"That view's commonplace for one with my might. And you stood there transfixed, like a brat."

The lawyer tried to think of a witty reply. He could not. He said, "Friend demon! Friend fat man! We must hurry! The shrink's beginning to remind me of a pig. And you both know what'll happen when I can't remember that he's a godlike man!"

The fat man yanked himself from his thoughts. "Uh, ahem, yes, you are quite correct. Demon. Demon? Come, come, my friend. We must keep our minds on the business at hand. Shrink, do not delay any longer. Get to it."

5. The eternal child awoke. He thought of the three godlike men who had listened so attentively to his cursing, then had so abruptly silenced him. He wondered where he was. At home? With the godlike men? Or was he outside,

lying on a golden sidewalk? Anxious for an answer, he opened his eyes, only to find himself blinded by darkness, deafened by a constant humming next to his ears. He tried to speak, but could not move his mouth. He tried to reach to his throat, but his hands felt as if they no longer existed. If he could have felt them, he would have clenched them or rubbed a surface, to see if he was imagining things, to see if all his nerves were really dead.

He felt himself drifting. Yet he somehow knew that he was lying on a cold, smooth surface. He listened to the constant humming, hoping to detect some noise underneath it which would give him a clue to where he was. Soon he thought he heard the muffled and distorted conversation of familiar voices, and at least he knew who was responsible for his stay in limbo.

Something happened to the eternal child. He changed. He knew it because he wanted with all his heart to curse in protest, and then, as he tried to open his mouth again, he realized the futility of cursing; not once had cursing resulted in communication that soothed the loneliness which consumed him. There had to be other ways. For an instant he yearned for the safe blackness of his parents' apartment, for the warm touch of their arms. Then he felt that no matter what was happening to him, he could overcome it without help. It was a foolish belief, of that he was sure, but self-confidence and courage smothered his fears.

The eternal child learned answers. Not to his current predicament, but to the predicament of his past life. He understood why his parents needed him, why they needed each other, what dirty jokes meant, why he was forever lonely, why he was an artificial child. He no longer hated female eternal children; instead, he felt a loss greater than any he had ever felt before, for he knew there would never be a female eternal child such as he to fill the chasm in his heart. He wondered how he could have thought that cursing the hawkman provided him with a sense of triumph. He realized that after the passing of childhood, mysteries always lingered, and certain memories and rationalizations were forever forgotten.

After the passing of childhood. Suddenly the mature eternal child knew everything. He surprised himself by not being afriad, by being glad. He wanted to see his parents again, for reasons different than before; he wanted them to be proud of him.

He felt his atoms break up, and he could not wait until he saw the world of godlike man through mature, preceptive eyes.

6. "Friend lawyer, please leave this most comfortable Morris chair," said the fat man, pulling off his white gloves and smiling with a satisfaction he had not felt in eons.

The lawyer's jaw dropped. "But your buttocks!"

"They are wide awake now and desperately need their eight hours."

Reluctantly the lawyer complied with the fat man's wishes. The demon had a mirthful look in his evil eyes as he watched the lawyer pace the room, searching among the many chairs for one even remotely as comfortable as the Morris chair. Brushing dust from his spats, the fat man said, "Friend lawyer, you should be more like the demon."

"I've tried sitting on the air. It pales compared to the Morris chair."

"And I have found that my buttocks pale without one. Withdrawal symptoms, I suppose."

"If you sat in the air, lawyer," said the demon, "you could fondle your peenie whenever you wanted to."

The lawyer snorted. "Why should I do that when I can twirl my sword-cane?"

"Godlike men such as you always prefer the symbol to the reality," said the demon.

"Speaking of reality has reminded me," said the fat man, "it is time to change the subject. We should be hearing from the gunsel soon. Already he is secreted in the proper apartment."

"With no chance of discovery?" asked the lawyer.

"Your foul mood has dimmed your powers of judgment considerably," replied the fat man.

The lawyer had no choice but to agree.

7. The mature eternal child had changed not only
mentally, but phsyically as well. After his atoms had re-
grouped outside the door to his parents' apartment, he inspected himself with a detachment he could only call unnatural under the circumstances. He wore black trousers, a
black shirt, and black shoes. His body was straight and
thin. Without looking at his face in a mirror, he knew he
had a weak chin; otherwise he was quite handsome, with
curly red hair covering his ears, with deep brown eyes and
high cheekbones. The floor was far away, but he was not
afraid; and he had no urge to get close to it. His powers of
perception had grown to such an extent that he realized he
was a true artist, not a game-player like his parents. Whatever identity the mature eternal child would assume in the
future, it would be one of his own making, not one taken
from the past.

He listened carefully for any sounds in the apartment.
He heard a soft voice, that of his mother. There was a note
of anxiety in it, as if she were gravely worried. Then he
heard his father say something in a comforting tone. The
mature eternal child realized—he didn't know how—that
his mother's worries were not eased.

His parents were concerned over his fate. That was the
most important thing a godlike man could be concerned
about—a missing eternal child. He wondered why he did
not enter immediately. And he wondered how he would
communicate with them, how he would explain the glorious
change that had come over him. He had never spoken anything but a curse before; now the urge to curse was gone
forever. He wondered if he should try to say something before he entered. No, his parents should have the privilege
of hearing his first true words.

He opened the door and saw his parents. His mother had
a streak of gray running through her hair; she wore a silver
gown; she sat on the couch, resting her elbows on her knees
and her head in her palms. She had been crying before, but
now all emotion was drained from her. His father wore a
black costume with a ruffled white shirt and black boots;

his features were soft, almost effeminate; he was dripping wet. He stood over his wife. He had evidently just given up trying to comfort her and was wondering what he should do next. They did not notice him.

The mature eternal child stepped inside the apartment. He said, "Mother," without thinking. His hands were clenched into fists, and he bit his lower lip. They seemed not to have heard him. He repeated the word.

His father looked at him. His father was at first confused and only gradually recognized the eternal child who was his adopted son. His jaw quivered as he searched for a suitable expression. But the mature eternal child did not notice the contortions of his father's face; he saw only the anger in his father's eyes.

His mother finally glanced at him. For an instant the mature eternal child felt the hope that he would gain immediate acceptance, that they would come to understand and be proud at once. For she was the one who knew: he was, in effect, their creation; and they had to face him. They could not turn away.

His mother looked toward the window. She spoke in a toneless voice. "Well? Are you happy? Your father died this morning, drowned in turbulent seas, and I could not mourn for him because I was so worried over your disappearance. How could you do such a thing?"

His father said, "He's just like all the other eternal children! We love him, clothe him, feed him, and house him. We created him! We justify him! And this is how he repays us! He ruins our whole day!"

The mature eternal child wanted to turn and run away from the apartment, but he knew that would not do; it would only delay the matter. "Don't you see how I've changed? I'm mature; I'm as intelligent as you; I don't have your powers, but in every other respect I'm your equal."

Shaking his fist, his father said, "Stop babbling nonsense! What did you run away for? Were your friends calling you? Or did you see that sorry hawkman?"

"Father, I swear it was none of my doing. The fat man and his friends are responsible."

"The fat man! He's powerless! Don't you think I know a lie when I hear one?"

"It's the truth, I swear it." The mature eternal child was

somewhat confused by the sound of his voice; it was a whine, so much like the mumbling he had used while he was a mere child. He was unnerved by his parents' reaction; they were not even surprised that he could talk as well as they. Saying the first words that came into his head, he was not remotely hinting at the vague speeches he had planned to use to make them understand.

His mother pondered the matter. "Well, dear, I suppose we could spank him and lock him in his room for a few days. Then you could drown yourself again in the turbulent seas and I could mourn for a few hours."

"No. It would seem empty and hopeless today. I think I should send him to the anti-matter universe and get another eternal child, one who would appreciate us."

The mature eternal child remembered that his father had said this a few times before, with the purpose of frightening him. But now the statement was an insult, and the mature eternal child lost all desire to control himself. His face turned red; he walked to his father and shook him; he said, "Look at me! Can't you see I'm different?"

His father lightly touched him to push him away. Then, staring at him, his father sat down and crossed his legs. "You're not acting normal. Are you sure you're well?"

"It must have been the hamburgers the clown gave him yesterday," his mother said. "Sometimes they do bad things to your stomach."

"No, it's not that! The hamburgers were good!" The mature eternal child looked away from his parents. He was acting the way they wanted him to. Forcing himself to calm down, he said slowly, as if he were trying to convince himself, "Listen to me. I'm different. I'm your son, but not in the same meaning of the word that I was yesterday. You must realize this."

"I realize that you've an upset stomach," said his mother. "We really must do something, mustn't we?"

"Suppose I ask the questions," said the mature eternal child, "and you answer me. Then maybe I can get to the bottom of this."

"If it's about your card deck, we put it in your room before I watched your father drown. I thought that if you came back in time for me to mourn, you would want it there."

"The questions are not about my card deck. I don't believe I'll ever need it again."

His father suddenly exploded in anger. "What do you mean you won't need it again? What kind of nonsense is that? You've always needed your card deck and you always will! I tell you, dear, it's time I trashed the living fire out of that boy!" His father stood up and took a few steps toward him.

But before his father could lay a hand on him, the mature eternal child shoved him back onto the couch. He said through his teeth, "If you try touching me again, you'll *have* to send me to the anti-matter universe, because I'll give you two black eyes. And the cattle baron doesn't have enough steers to keep the swelling down. Understand?"

His father did not react. His mother cried. "It's true," she said, "it's true! He's mad! We'll have to get another eternal child."

"You may have to find a replacement for me, but not before you answer my questions."

"Poppycock!" said his father. "What kind of questions do you think you could ask?"

"Have I ever asked questions before?"

"Of course not," his father replied. "You were content to accept things as they were."

"And the fact that I'm not content any longer must tell you something, mustn't it?"

"Just that you're sick," said his mother.

"What do I look like?" asked the mature eternal child, standing straight, with his arms at his side, looking above them at a painting of the sea.

"He does seem to be a little bit taller," said his mother. "Do you think he and his friends have found a rack somewhere and started playing with it?"

"When did you wash your face?" asked his father. "You know we like your face to be dirty."

"My face will be clean from now on."

"Not if I have anything to do with it," said his father, conjuring mud from nothingness and flinging it at his child.

The mature eternal child sidestepped the mud with ease. "I've said that I was going to keep clean, and I will. From now on I've something to say about what I do and what I look like."

"Not a chance," said his father.

"And don't go holding your breath until you turn blue," said his mother. "You know how it upsets the delicate artificial organs inside you."

"He'll calm down after he holds his breath a few times and realizes how useless it is," said his father. "But what does he want?"

"I want you to understand that I'm no longer the child who needs cards, or needs to hold his breath. I'm different now."

"I didn't know our son had a sense of humor," said his mother. "I think he's trying to play a joke on us. By talking and that sort of thing."

"I don't think he's ever had one," said his father, "so it can't be that. Where did we go wrong?"

"Well, we have to punish him somehow," said his mother. "His behavior is simply unseemly, uncustomary."

His father rubbed his chin and stared at his silent, unmoving son. "You know, dear, there *is* something different about him after all. He appears desperate and overwrought. Perhaps his friends have been giving him a hard time."

"I don't have any friends," said the mature eternal child quietly. "And I suppose I never will unless you understand."

"There isn't much to understand," said his mother. "Just that you're sick. Why don't you go to your room and play cards until you go to sleep? Then we can discuss it tomorrow morning before your father drowns."

He left them sitting and walked to his room. It seemed that they would never understand, that they would forever regard him as the helpless child of old. He realized that he never shoud have returned. He should have found an identity and home for himself without their approval. He should have been forever lost to them. Yet if he had done that, his achievements would have been meaningless. He still would have felt empty and without hope.

Inside his room he realized how small it really was. The blackness did not represent safety; it was confining. He sat down on the bed, looked at the floor, and listened to the voices of his parents. Somehow he would convince them and make them proud of him (he believed that even though he knew it was hopeless). It was the only satisfying path open to him. He knew he would succeed. He had forever.

8. The dapper young lawyer paced the room. He tried to twirl his sword-cane, but his hands shook nervously and he always dropped it. "When's he coming back? How long can the fat man talk to his gunsel and sustain the incredible suspense I'm undergoing?"

Pouring butter over popcorn, the demon said, "As long as he wants."

The lawyer snorted in disgust. "Some comfort you are!" He sat in the Morris chair. "This is unbearable!"

"Perhaps the little affair we've engineered has a complicated outcome." He tossed a kernel into his beak.

"Complicated, be damned! Either we get depression or we don't."

The fat man entered without knocking, tossing his Borsalino on the horn of Behemoth. Walking past the demon, he took a great handful of buttered popcorn. "I have returned," he said in his most pompous voice. He ate the popcorn in one gulp.

The lawyer stood up in his anxiousness to hear what the fat man had to say. "Quick! Your report! Your report!"

"I report that the outcome of the little affair we have engineered is complicated, and I do not know what to make of it. We have reaped confusion, anger, and a few other things, but no depression. The final results will not be in for a few million years or so." He wiped the grease from his hand with his white handkerchief; he teleported his handkerchief to the laundry bag in the guest room.

"I can't wait that long!" said the lawyer. "Kitty may have found somebody else by then!"

"If she can't in a few million years," said the demon, "then she will go the way of mere man."

"For all practical intents and purposes," said the fat man, nudging the lawyer away from the Morris chair, "we have failed. At the moment I am at a loss for schemes."

"But we'll try again?" asked the lawyer, visions of Kitty numbing his brain.

"Of course," said the demon, picking up a kernel with

his sticky forked tongue. "We've forever if we want it. I, for one, will take it."

The fat man nodded his approval. Beaming, the lawyer shouted, "All for depression! And depression for all!"

SLICES OF LIFE:
TWO

On Earth an entire continent was reserved for hunting. The portly author teleported himself all over Africa, shooting a cigar-smoking frog here, disintegrating a woolly mammoth there, and riding friendly chimeras everywhere. Whenever he killed an animal, he immediately brought it back to life—unless he was drunk and forgot. Tourists and hunters took photos of the many wonderful and exotic animals of Africa—of flocks of passenger pigeons, of flying leopards, of tigers and dinosaurs, of stone animals, and of two-dimensional animals. They marveled at the palm trees, the walking cacti, the humming underbrush, and the seed-spitting balls of green fur. They enjoyed the heavy daily rainfall, the scorching sun, the barren golden desert, and the brisk fresh air. Many were appalled by the savagery they deemed necessary to preserve the balance of life—whatever *that* was—but they were fascinated by it too.

There was one godlike man who was tired of the balance of life. "I'm fed up with it." he always said. "If those plants and animals want to kill each other, why can't they do it on their own? Why do they need me to oversee it? After all, they seem like they could do pretty well without me." The godlike man was correct in that respect; he was only an administrator. But the delicate balance of life could be tipped over by any of the various creatures that populated Africa —especially the intelligent cigar-smoking frogs whose one purpose in life, it seemed, was to cause trouble for their kind-hearted administrator. He had to keep his eyes on them all the time; he could not even enjoy the rainbow mountains which from a distance proved to be gigantic effigies of famous godlike men and women in compromising positions—pornographic mountains, a personal creation which only he could recognize because only he knew from where and from how high up to look at the rainbow mountains so the picture became obvious. The mountains were his huge private joke upon his world, the one object that prevented his love for Africa from turning into a bitter, dry emotion. But no, he could not enjoy even that. He had to spend too much time watching out for those cigar-smoking frogs.

The godlike administrator of Africa was known simply as—the duck.

The duck was half a meter tall, with huge, yellow, flat feet that made a slapping noise when he walked upright in his treehouse. His hands had four fingers. His eyes were large ovals; they appeared to have been drawn above his huge, yellow, flat beak. His feathers were pure white. He wore spats and a blue jacket. He had no genitals; he knew that if the time ever came when he needed them, he could create them on the spot. Any spot. He experienced a peculiar tingling, like a tiny explosion inside his body, whenever he looked at the pornographic rainbow mountains, but that was, he told himself, only his artistic pride acting up again.

The duck's greatest pleasure in life was sleeping late; then he dreamed of the walking cacti multiplying a thousandfold and chasing the frogs all over the continent. One morning as he slept, dreaming of the frogs being tortured by listening to the Big Red Cheese telling of his most daring exploits, his right-hand assistant, known as the mouse, crept into his treehouse.

"Get up, you eggsucker!" said the mouse in his squeaky voice. The mouse had two large round ears resembling discuses. He was completely black save for a white snout with a black tip. He wore red trunks and white four-fingered gloves. The duck had no idea if the mouse had genitals, nor did he know what the mouse's feet looked like; the mouse never took off his large wooden shoes in the presence of the duck. The mouse was a particularly disgusting vision to behold first thing in the morning, and the duck told him so in no uncertain terms.

"Do you think I like looking at *you*?" asked the mouse. "I'd be in bed, too, but an emergency is developing."

"Don't tell me."

"You guessed it; the cigar-smoking frogs."

The duck nodded, for once the mouse had acted correctly. Only the duck was capable of handling the cigar-smoking frogs, which was why they caused him so much trouble. Frogs had their pride, too, especially intelligent ones whose major cause of death was lung cancer. He got out of bed, shined his spats, dressed, and under the mouse's guidance, teleported to the troubled site.

The duck and the mouse stood on a high yellow peak in the rainbow mountains. The duck suffered an anxiety attack; had the frogs finally discovered his one weak spot? If they had, then surely his life would crumble into ashes, he thought, admonishing himself for looking at the matter the way the mouse would have.

The mouse silently, grimly pointed toward a green mountain. Hidden among the green trees and bushes, and behind the green boulders, were the frogs. The duck rubbed the bottom of his flat beak. Soon some frogs boldly stepped out of hiding and squatted in the open, as if they were innocently resting after a long hike. The frogs were not unhandsome creatures, considering the ugliness of ther ancestors. Although bow-legged, with all four thin limbs appearing frail enough to be crushed and broken by the mildest accident, their posture was excellent, their shoulders always thrown back. Their webbed feet provided them with good support; their webbed hands were powerful and versatile. Their features—flat noses and wide mouths—and their pale green complexions never varied; the duck was able to recognize their leader, Queen Elda, only by her silver crown, though it was said that the frogs never had trouble telling each other apart; they were even able to recognize a friend from a distance. They were not smoking their stinking cigars; they never smoked them when they were bothering the duck. They strutted proudly, from hiding place to hiding place, like the true conquerers they believed themselves to be. Their legends told them that a day would come when

71

godlike mankind would leave Earth, and the planet would be theirs. It was their destiny.

The duck gave the walking cacti a better chance of inheriting the Earth then he did the cigar-smoking frogs. "What are they doing?" he asked the mouse.

The mouse shrugged. "I don't know," he squeaked.

"Then I guess the only thing to do is to hide and wait and let them make the first move."

The duck and the mouse secreted themselves behind a yellow tree. The duck's attention wandered; he stared at the azure sky and the thin clouds shielding the sun. He also stared at the yellow ground and at the purple mountains above the green mountain inhabited by the frogs. He wondered exactly where he was in his huge effigy. Was he sitting up someone's nostril? Was he part of a chest? Lips? Feet? He did not dwell upon the subject for long; there were many portions of godlike bodies he did not want to be sitting in.

After an hour—by now the sun was stark—the mouse touched the duck on the shoulder. He pointed at the frogs: some were obscured by dust. They dragged machinery the duck could not recognize from the underbrush. When the dust settled and all the frogs, including Queen Elda, and the machinery were clearly in view, the duck understood for the first time what the frogs were up to.

"Those are gatling guns!" exclaimed the mouse.

"No kidding," said the duck, putting a finger to his beak, signalling the mouse to be quiet.

"What do you think they're up to?" whispered the mouse.

"I don't know. I'm only an underrated civil servant trying to do my job."

"Didn't I do good to wake you up? I told you something was brewing. Didn't I do good?"

"You did good. Now shut up."

"Look!" said the mouse, pointing at the foot of the green mountain.

The duck saw the portly author, staggering about in a drunken stupor and drinking from a liquor bottle. As soon as he finished the contents of the bottle, the portly author collapsed and passed out. The duck looked to the frogs. The frogs aimed the gatling guns at the portly author.

Queen Elda raised her thin arm. When she brought it down, the frogs would open fire.

The duck did not know if godlike men could die; no one had ever been in such a situation before. He wanted to send the frogs to the anti-matter universe, but that would upset Africa's precious balance of life; there would be no one to eat the glowing flies which would infest the continent. There was only one line of action left open to him. (Of course, the duck might be able to heal the portly author, to return him to life, but, again, that had never been done to a godlike man before.)

The duck sent the gatling guns to the anti-matter universe.

Their mouths agape, the frogs stared at where the guns had been. They looked to Queen Elda; their confused expressions were silent questions of what to do next. Before Queen Elda could instruct her subjects, the duck and mouse floated from concealment and landed on the green mountain above the frogs.

"You . . . you . . . you . . ." said Queen Elda in a musical, lovely voice which was the envy of godlike women everywhere, "you're always in the way!"

"Cool it!" shouted the mouse.

"I second the motion," said the duck. "Just what did you frogs expect to prove anyway?"

"Africa is ours!" said Queen Elda. "Africa for the frogs!"

"Africa for the frogs!" chorused her subjects.

"Africa is for the godlike men, of which I'm a supreme example," said the duck. "You nits are powerless before me. Now go home. I'm bored."

Mumbling among themselves, the frogs did as they were told, keeping their distance from the unconscious portly author. The duck knew he would not have any more trouble from the cigar-smoking frogs for a few days. As soon as they were out of his sight, they would light up, get into their jeeps, and drive home. Then they would sleep, eat glowing flies, relax, and stay up late scheming. By this time the duck knew their *modus operandi* well.

When they heard the gentle hum of the jeeps and saw dust rising in the distance, the duck and the mouse floated to the portly author. They briefly inspected him to see if he had injured himself; he had not, and they teleported him home.

Despite himself, the duck was proud that he had thwarted the frogs. Although their mission had not been directly associated with the balance of life they were bent upon destroying, it had been an act of revenge. And he had once again stung their pride. It was a good feeling, winning every time.

After giving the mouse instructions to have spies watch the frogs just in case their attempt on the portly author's life had been a diversion, the duck teleported to the treehouse and went to sleep. His dreams were full of fame and glory. The next time he defeated the cigar-smoking frogs, the race of godlike men would know how competent the dynamic administrator of Africa was.

CHAPTER THREE

1. The yellow pigs in trench coats awoke early every morning to pull weeds and to pick ripe vegetables, corn and beans, for the godlike men who did not wish to waste precious energy for their food. The pigs drank beer and wine while working; usually they passed out midway through the afternoon. Sometimes, as a pig lay on his back, his eyes half-closed, his thoughts muddled by alcohol and exhaustion, he saw a tiny black figure silhouetted against the sun. It seemed to the pig that the godlike man was experiencing joy. The godlike man flew in great arcs; he flew to the upper regions of the atmosphere; he dropped as if he were falling, and then pulled himself out, cutting another arc. Gradually he was lost to the pig's sight. The pig was glad; following the black figure against the bright sun, while in a drunken stupor, was making him sick.

The pig would not have cared that in reality the godlike man was *not* experiencing joy; if the demon, the lawyer, and the fat man had known, they would have applauded gleefully. For this godlike man was the lonely hawkman, who did not fly with the power of thought, but through the use of his anti-gravity belt. His great gray wings allowed him to control the direction of his flight. Like all godlike men of his type, his costume looked as if it had been painted on. The hawkman wore no shirt, just yellow straps to hold on his wings. He wore red tights and green boots. His orange mask was designed to resemble the visage of a hawk; at the ears were wings; the eyes looked as if they

75

were placed at his temples. Flying was his only hope to forget his loneliness, his belief that he had been born in the wrong time. That hope was never fulfilled; but he always flew.

One day he decided to fly all over the Earth to see if he would be lucky enough to find any other relics of the past to place in Carter Hall; just an eon ago he had found an ancient can-opener. He flew over his nameless native city, which housed one-third of the godlike men in golden apartment complexes or in suburban areas. The hawkman wondered how they could tolerate living so close together when they had the entire Earth, the entire universe to explore. (And why didn't he explore the universe? he asked himself. Carter Hall, he answered.) On the outskirts of the city grew dense green forests, with trees hundreds of years old, and with much younger trees feeding from soil made damp and dark by the rotting remains of the older, dead drees. To his right, far below him, there was a huge cluster of trees which had grown for several millenia and showed no signs of ever dying. Only one godlike man lived among them, in a two bedroom treehouse; he traveled forever in the wrong direction and he yearned for the lovely princess in his garden. The hawkman scowled beneath his mask. Even that godlike man, blessed by the glories of nature, swore that he would one day renounce his identity and become a pirate in the most unusual airship he could design.

Hovering above the cluster of giant trees, the hawkman wondered if anyone else would occupy the treehouse afterward. He realized there was no use in pondering the question; he had no logical means of obtaining an answer, and he doubted he had the power to find one intuitively.

He sighted a flock of birds in the distance. He caught up with them and gave them the power to speak his language fluently. He did it often, to see if he could accidently establish a basis for kinship with them that would ease the loneliness he felt. But as usual the birds could not grasp the concepts behind the words; they babbled the words, ran them together without a thought of making them mean anything. The hawkman decided once again that it was best if they stuck to their songs, which were lonely and heartbreaking, and he took the power of words away from them.

Then he flew to the only seriously high mountain range

in the hemisphere. A thick blanket of snow covered the barren summits. He watched his breath swirl and dissolve in the thin air. He glided as much as possible: it was painful to inhale; the air felt like icicles in his lungs. He wondered if he should warm himself by thought. However, the basis for his identity had not done that, so he decided that he also should not.

He watched two green rams battle for a mate, and the echoes of their blows rang in his ears long after they had faded from the mountain passes.

He saw the invisible abominable godlike man make footprints in the snow; it looked as if he were happily skipping toward some unknown destination.

The hawkman wondered why he had bothered to make the journey at all; he knew as well as anyone that there were no more relics of the past left to be discovered. They were all in Carter Hall. All. He had placed them there himself.

Giving up on his quest, he flew to the sea. And, as usual, he came closer to peace than ever before. Of all the changes Earth had undergone since the rise of the godlike men eons ago, only the sea had remained untouched. The sea was always the same. From above he watched the green waters ripple. He sniffed the salt in the air as he swooped downward and straightened out just two meters above the sea. He slowed his flight so he could catch glimpses of fish leaping in the air or the swish of their tails as they dove deep, deep into the waters.

When he was close to the sea, the hawkman could always vividly imagine the Earth as it was before. Then he had had people to talk to: a wife who had shared his life and adventures; a police commissioner far away in the stars to whom he had reported; and a very tiny man who had been his best friend.

All of Earth's secrets had been planted in his unconscious.

And he had had a cause; he had fought evil everywhere, in all its manifestations; goodness, represented by himself, had always triumphed.

But those days were gone forever. Now he was only the lonely hawkman, a collector of battered television sets, rusty soup cans, old smelly tires, and other artifacts which his instincts told him had originated eons ago.

Of all godlike men, only his dreams remained dreams.

Inevitably, his thoughts became too crushing to bear, and not even the sea was a comfort. He flew straight toward Carter Hall.

He did not glance down when he flew over the barren tundra, nor at the tiny village of redneck godlike men, nor at the angry old author (with one classic book to his credit) making a bad movie with actors who did not like him.

He detoured once: to avoid the mysterious ivory tower that soared loftily into unmoving white clouds that clung forever to it; the tower was surrounded by black orchids that made him want to sneeze; they made him strangely nervous. He sped past quickly.

The hawkman looked forward to resting in Carter Hall, cluttered and uncomfortable as it was with boxes of artifacts for which he had no room on the shelves, with its restored statues, with its musty air and boarded windows.

When he was five kilometers from his native city, something stirred inside the hawkman; his instincts told him to look below. His face beneath the mask turned red and his breath came in gasps. The hawkman realized that his chances of success were slim; his instincts had been always wrong recently; but he had to slow down and follow his instincts, nonetheless.

He saw the godlike man with no name, riding a mule and lighting a cigar stub. His green poncho was dusty and so were his boots ad black hat. The godlike man was alone, as always. He liked it that way.

Normally the hawkman would have left it that way. The godlike man with no name seethed with an anger about to explode. The hawkman knew he was being foolhardy, even as he glided into the proper position to carry out the plan which had occurred to him.

A kilometer behind the godlike man with no name, the hawkman flapped his great gray wings as fast as he could, supplementing the tremendous wind he created with power from his own mind. He flew toward his prey, calculating that if he stayed twenty meters above the ground it would look like an accident when the wind knocked the godlike man with no name from his mule.

The plan succeeded with a snag. The godlike man with no name was sucked upward by the wind, flew fifteen meters, collided with a tree before he could stop himself, cursed, fell, rolled, and stood up, throwing one end of his poncho over his shoulder to expose his weapons.

The hawkman tried to hide his disappointment as he approached the godlike man with no name. His instincts had indeed been wrong. The hawkman had hoped to see two ancient, rusty Colt .45's riding on the godlike man's thighs; instead, he saw facsimiles, mere props that channeled the power of thought. Now the only thing left for him to do was to carry out the charade.

"I'm sorry," said the hawkman, trying to sound apologetic. "I didn't see you."

The godlike man with no name took his dusty cigar stub from his mouth, rolled it between his thumb and forefinger, and said, "Yeah," in a gravelly, whispery voice.

"I'm sorry," said the hawkman. "I really am."

The godlike man with no name remained silent. He squinted again.

The hawkman created a black shade which shielded them from the harsh sunlight. The godlike man with no name was still silent. "Look," said the hawkman, "I'm sorry. If there's anything that I can do. . . ."

The godlike man with no name took off his hat and brushed it on his pants. Staring at the hawkman, he put his cigar stub back into his mouth. He turned away and walked toward his mule.

The hawkman smiled to himself. It was as if the incident were already forgotten. He had found no relic, but he would get over that soon enough. He spread his wings and flew up into the waiting sky; he watched the shade disintegrate from above. Maybe he would fly around a while before returning to Carter Hall. Maybe he would try to talk to the birds again.

2. The fat man puffed his pipe; the smoke smelled like sweaty gym socks. The demon floated about his apartment and whisked dust to the anti-matter universe. They

had not spoken all morning; both pretended to be deep in thought, mulling over potential schemes. Occasionally the fat man took his pipe from his mouth and rolled his eyes toward the ceiling, as if he was about to speak. But he only shifted his weight in the Morris chair and blew silver smoke-rings. Sometimes the demon raised his finger and nipped at it with his yellow beak, but then he shook his head and rubbed his chin, being careful not to scratch his delicate skin with his sharp fingernails.

At noon the demon grew tired of the silence and said, "Must that smoke smell so foul?"

The fat man chuckled. "I am fond of it."

The demon sighed and said, "Why don't you make it smell like something decent?"

"You mean like fragile red roses, or like an early spring morning, heavy with the scent of dew?"

"No. Like the charred remains of an offering to the devil, or like the sulfurous stench of some nameless god from another dimension. That sort of thing."

The fat man laughed deep in his stomach. "No, no, my friend, I do not think I can do that."

"I didn't think you could, but it didn't hurt to ask."

"Do you think it would hurt if I asked where the lawyer is?"

The demon glared at a mirror. The mirror cast no reflection of the demon. "I'll hurt *him* if he doesn't show up soon."

At that moment the lawyer entered, slamming the door behind him and tossing his derby on a horn of Behemoth. "Friend fat man, I must insist that you find another place for your gunsel to sleep!"

The fat man raised an inquisitive eyebrow.

The lawyer pointed at the fat man with his sword-cane; his knuckles were red and the veins in his neck stood out as if they were about to burst. He stammered a few incomprehensible words; he ran his fingers through his hair, lowering his sword-cane for only a second. However, he dropped the sword-cane when he noticed that a generous sampling of greasy hair tonic was smeared on his hand. He waved the greasy hand next to his black silk suit and pulled a pink silk handkerchief from his pocket with his clean hand. After he was finished with the handkerchief, he snuffed it out of existence. By this time he was calm enough to speak. "Now don't get me wrong. I don't want you to get me wrong."

Looking at the demon, the fat man rolled his eyes, assuming a why-me appearance.

"Just promise me that you won't get me wrong," continued the lawyer.

"I promise," said the fat man.

"Your gunsel is getting on my nerves, but I don't want you to think that I don't like him. Why, I've never said a word to him in my life, and I've only caught a few glimpses of him all the time he's been staying with me."

"Please, friend lawyer, don't feel lonely," said the demon. "You can always talk to us."

"That's not what I'm getting at! I'm trying to tell you that every morning when I get up, things are missing or misplaced, and it's bothering me. It's bothering me a lot, now that I think about it. Dirty dishes are always in the living room; the water is running; stains are on the tables and rugs; and books have torn jackets. My apartment is breaking into tiny little pieces! I tell you, the gunsel is not making me happy!"

"It would appear that you are not having any trouble at all telling us this," said the fat man, conjuring a glass of lemonade for the lawyer.

"Besides, why should he make you happy?" asked the demon.

"Somebody has to! Kitty certainly isn't!"

"Aha!" said the fat man. "Now we come to the problem's root."

"Watch your mouth," said the lawyer.

The fat man sighed as if he had been suffering all his life. "Please, friend lawyer, you have angered me enough today by being late; you know I detest tardiness. And you know I dislike it when you allow your love life, or lack of it, to affect your usually extraordinary sense of manners and good taste. I could not be more fond of my gunsel if he were my own eternal child, so please, enough of this madness. We have plans to make."

The lawyer calmed himself with a visible effort. "Yes. I suppose you're correct."

"You may do more than suppose," said the fat man confidently. "The only reason I have been wrong in the recent

81

past is because I am not yet used to playing in the big leagues. I will get over that soon."

"There's much pride in your voice," said the lawyer sarcastically, clearly in no mood to agree with the fat man on any issue.

"And rightly so. But, friend lawyer, in your own way you have managed to bring us to the point again. I admire you for your succinctness."

The lawyer smiled despite himself; receiving a compliment always brightened his day. "Oh, thank you. But what's the point?"

"The point is—" said the demon and the fat man at once. The fat man waved his hand, deferring to the other.

"The point is that there's too much pride in our race," said the demon. "Godlike men have too much pride in their carefree existence to be depressed over anything. Before depression can return, pride must be eradicated."

"Once and for all?" asked the lawyer.

"For a little while will do," said the fat man, emptying his pipe in a silver ashtray. "When a sense of pride returns, godlike men will fight the depression they believe is destroying them. Which, after all, is what we want."

The lawyer paced about the room. He bumped into a table, but ignored the brief jab of pain. He slipped on his sword-cane, but did not fall. Picking up his sword-cane, he said, "And just how do you propose to eradicate pride?"

Shrugging, the fat man said, "The details have not been worked out. We shall not know until late tonight."

"Why not?"

The fat man smiled at the demon, who nodded in approval. "He really is succinct today, like a man possessed," said the fat man. "Do you really suppose that he no longer feels mere desire for Kitty, that some deeper emotion has seized him?"

"There's that possibility," said the demon.

"Why not?"

The fat man chuckled. "Each member of our race takes great pride in being a godlike man; with good reason, I might add. Rarely does a godlike man contemplate his origins. Why not? The answer is that he does not want to be reminded of them. Mere man is spoken of with disdain and hatred. The demon and I have decided that a propaganda campaign is in order, that we should seek to gradually force godlike men to remember the truth. To do so we must learn more of the truth for ourselves. Tonight we must go to Carter Hall . . . when the hawkman is asleep; and we can work without disturbance."

3. Few places in the golden city were shunned by the godlike men, and they were shunned not because of fear, but because there was no reason or desire to visit them. Such a place was gray Carter Hall. The hawkman spent his days alone, leaving his home only to fly or to search for relics. At home he tried to piece together as much history as he could, reading old books and trying to learn the purpose behind many items. He realized that he was consumed by passion for a few insignificant seconds in the history of the universe, and learning the truth about those few seconds was incredibly difficult; so many trivial events had occurred, so many worthless inventions had been built, and so many unimaginative words had been spoken. The hawkman comprehended little of it, but mere man was more than a hobby to him; the race was the only possible justification for the hawkman's existence. Consequently the hawkman studied with a diligence alien to most of his kind.

He always studied late into the night, sitting at a golden desk, with one lamp turned on; he leaned his wings against the stone wall behind him, and his mask was on the floor next to his wooden chair. He held an object carefully, close to his eyes, scrutinizing every minute detail. His forehead was wrinkled more than it should have been, as if he believed someone was watching him and he wanted the intruder to know how hard he was concentrating. The hawkman rarely admitted to himself that soon after midnight his mind wandered; it was easier to think of the entirety of mere man's history rather than of a particular; it was much more interesting and exciting. He wished he could learn everything at once, and sometimes, while wishing, he looked up from the object and gazed into the blackness surrounding him. He looked outside and saw more blackness—relieved only by the tiny light of the stars.

And he imagined the blackness to be inside himself, a vast pit in his heart and stomach. Usually, he was able to bring back his mind to the particular object he was studying; if not, he decided he was sleepy and went to bed.

The night after the hawkman had encountered the godlike man with no name was no exception. He went to bed just after midnight, and before he closed his eyes to sleep, he turned off the remaining lights in Carter Hall and the machinery that manufactured musty air: the appropriate air for a museum of the past. He turned it off with a thought.

Shunned Carter Hall became part of the night itself.

It was surrounded by the rubble of golden apartment buildings that had been mysteriously torn down eons ago. (Not even the hawkman could remember why; not that he gave the matter much thought; one morning the people had moved and the buildings had been found lying all over the streets, that was all.) Carter Hall had some small resemblance to the churches and synagogues where the various godlike priests and rabbis lived, searching for someone who was as good and noble and selfless as themselves; but Carter Hall had steel bars instead of stained glass windows; there was litter in the yard and on the steps; and there were no golden stone gargoyles overlooking the roof's edge. Carter Hall was crumbling; it would have taken just a thought to mend it, but the hawkman savored its decadent atmosphere; it evoked thoughts of a time when everything eventually fell apart. Columns had cracked in half and rolled across the street; the sidewalk had gaping holes filled with stagnant rain water; the front door creaked when it was opened. The hawkman would have been pleased if he had known of the stories eternal children told each other of the decrepit building—it was haunted by the ghosts of mere men; an eternal child who went there was always crippled, somehow, in some fashion. The few godlike men who had heard these tales scoffed, calling them simple fancy. The lawyer had once called them that, too, but tonight he viewed the matter differently.

The lawyer walked beside the fat man; floating above them, the demon searched for a signal from the gunsel. The fat man whistled tunelessly. The lawyer stared at Carter Hall for a while, then lowered his eyes toward the golden sidewalk, watching his feet take each step, until he began to lose his equilibrium. He twirled his sword-cane so he would have something to do with his hands. His mind dwelled upon the mysteries he and his friends would soon discover, but he tried to think of other things; he could not; his mind always drew back to Carter Hall. The lawyer could not explain why his heart was beating so fiercely; it seemed that he looked at the night through a haze. Briefly, he thought of what he had seen in the thirty-second dimension, and of what he had felt; he wondered if Carter Hall would inspire such awe. As soon as he realized that he was simply afraid, the lawyer decided that the demon and the fat man should not even remotely suspect the truth.

"Where's the gunsel?" he demanded. "What's keeping that little shrimp?"

"Quiet!" said the fat man. "We must be quiet!" It suddenly dawned upon him that he had been speaking almost as loud as the lawyer; he groaned and whispered, "We must wait. Be patient. And do not worry about what Kitty is doing tonight; what she is doing is ignoring you."

Before the lawyer could reply, the demon said, "The gunsel'll let us know when the hawkman's asleep. Then I shall place a spell on him that'll keep him that way."

"But why did we even have to wait until tonight?" asked the lawyer, hoping that he was not revealing his dark secret. "We could have searched just as well in the daytime."

"You would prefer that we waited until tomorrow?" asked the fat man.

The lawyer stopped himself from answering just in time.

"I don't believe that the hawkman would allow us to 'borrow' some of his relics," said the demon. "He certainly is weird."

"All right. I understand," said the lawyer. "I just want to get this over with, that's all."

The trio turned a corner. Three blocks away was the huge entrance to Carter Hall. The lawyer stubbed his toe on a golden brick. "Ow! Why doesn't someone clean this place up?"

"Nobody every comes here," said the demon.

"Nobody in his right mind, anyway," mumbled the lawyer.

A shrill whistle sounded in the darkness. The lawyer imagined the fat man smiling in satisfaction.

"That, friend lawyer," said the fat man, "was my gunsel's signal."

"You could have fooled me," said the lawyer.

The fat man bowed gracefully. "You may proceed me."

"Thank you," said the lawyer, trying to shed the nagging suspicion that the only reason the fat man was allowing him to go first was that anything bad that happened would happen to *him* first.

The lawyer and the fat man walked without speaking, the demon still floating above them. The lawyer wondered how the fat man's steps could be so silent, with all his immense weight behind them, and how the imposing sounding-board of Carter Hall could be echoing the tapping of his own steps. He lifted himself three millimeters from the sidewalk, but the resulting total silence did not comfort him. He watched the sidewalk glide past him.

"Oh no," said the demon.

"Oh no," said the fat man.

"What the —" said the lawyer, looking up. "Oh no."

The lights of Carter Hall were on.

"Friend demon, is the hawkman still asleep?" asked the fat man. "He might have had to go to the, uh, the, uh."

"He's asleep like an eternal child," said the demon. "I didn't even have to cast my spell."

"He must have had a hard day," said the lawyer. He smiled to himself. "Well, I guess that's it. The lights are on. We can't go in."

"I don't know about that," said the demon. "We would have turned them on anyway."

"But someone's in there," said the lawyer. "We'll be caught."

"Nonsense," said the fat man, just before he puffed out of sight. Only a thin wisp of red smoke remained.

"Now where did he go?" asked the lawyer, pacing about in a circle.

"To speak to his gunsel, I would imagine," said the demon, drifting closer to the ground and turning his head completely around, hoping to catch sight of the fat man.

The fat man materialized in front of them. "I have completed speaking to my gunsel. He informs me that no one has entered the building. The lights probably came on by accident."

"Look!" said the lawyer. "I saw someone! A shadowy figure passed by that window! That one there!"

"Nonsense," said the fat man. "My gunsel is never wrong."

"If it was anyone—which I doubt—it was the postman, delivering the mail a little bit early," quipped the demon. "Let's go."

Chuckling, the fat man began walking toward Carter Hall to show that he considered the conversation closed. Catching flies with his tongue, the demon floated behind him. The lawyer was thankful for one thing; he was now behind the others. He wondered if he was being foolish; his friends were extremely confident and he had every reason to trust them. Or were their thoughts the same as his? Were they hiding their fear? As they neared Carter Hall, the blackness surrounding them becoming diminished by the light inside, the lawyer decided that it did not matter.

They slowly walked up the long path of golden steps leading to the front doors, as if they wanted to savor the joys of nearing a goal as long as possible. The fat man, a giant mushroom in the darkness, swayed back and forth. The demon breathed fire as if he were relishing the last smoke drawn from a pipe.

The demon reached the entrance first. His green skin was pale under the yellow light spilling from the cracked and broken windows and between the rusty bars. He clapped his hands, as he often did while casting a spell, and the doors of Carter Hall creaked open. The fat man chuckled in satisfaction; the lawyer took a step backward, cringing, fully expecting to be faced with some monster bent upon his destruction. Instead he was struck with a gush of foul air. He turned his head and coughed.

The demon inhaled deeply. "This air's even better than that of the shrink's laboratory," he said. "Just as I imagine the smell of Hell to be. Don't you think so, friend lawyer?"

The lawyer coughed again. "Freshen it up."

The demon looked disappointed. "But I love to smell air like this. I always have to smell fresh, healthy air. A godlike man gets tired of living in an eternal springtime. I want to smell air that fogs the eyes, clogs the lungs, and makes the nose drip."

"Are you serious?" asked the lawyer.

"I am afraid he is," said the fat man. "A strange opinion for someone with four nostrils, no doubt about it. But do not worry; the air shall eventually freshen up. And in the meantime I shall conjure gas masks for us." He did, making his own three times larger than the lawyer's so it would accommodate the immensity of his face.

The lawyer accepted his gas mask with a silent nod of thanks.

They entered, the demon first, the fat man second, and the lawyer lagging behind. The hallway was jammed with wooden crates of relics and statues and glass cases protecting fragile objects from decay. There was some small order to the jamming; the hawkman had made sure there were paths for him to walk through and room for him to fly above the boxes. The lawyer walked about; the fat man was forced to float beside the demon because his width was greater than even the span of the hawkman's folded wings.

"Just what are we looking for?" asked the lawyer.

"I do not know," said the fat man. "But I will when I find it."

"Look for anything that might be of vital importance to our cause," said the demon.

Since they were forced to conduct their search from above, the demon and the fat man used energy to peer inside the wooden crates. Separating, they floated from cramped room to cramped room. They read old books in a matter of seconds; they deduced the purposes of engines (they were much smarter than the hawkman); they examined dishes and bowls; they discovered the puzzling remains of advertising billboards; they saw old road signs; they practiced their arithmetic by determining if the figures in old accounting books were correct. Once, when both were in the same room, the fat man exclaimed, "Why, here is a corporation that failed because its lackeys could not juggle the books with an ounce of imagination!"

The demon nodded solemnly. "I'm glad we value fame and glory more than we value gold."

"So am I; if we valued gold, even the poorest of us

would be rich, and then what would be the point of being rich?"

"Of course, by our standards, we're poor."

"Do not remind me," said the fat man, resting his hands on his stomach. "But bad days will pass. Bad days always pass. It seems, however, that all our bad days have been coming in a row."

They separated again, still searching for the discovery from the past that would provide the key to glorious depression.

The lawyer, feeling extremely contrary, decided to search in a more physical manner; he found an ancient, rusty crowbar and, holding his sword-cane under his arm, pried open crates. Sometimes the crates were taller than him, and he had to grab the edges and lift himself up to peer inside. Usually he scraped his fingers while dropping back and he had to do away with the splinters sticking from his palms. He was still frightened that the hawkman would awake and discover them, but the sounds of his friends laughing over some relic eventually comforted him, and he came to share their apparent confidence. Soon, he too smiled; he threw away his gas mask, as had the fat man; more than once he called them over to examine a particulary hilarious relic of mere man. "It's hard to believe," he told them, "that such a primitive and frivolous race could have given birth to the glorious godlike men."

"But you must remember that the godlike men have yet to live up to their potential," said the fat man.

"I remember," said the lawyer. "And so would the rest of the world if we forced the people, one by one, to this Carter Hall. They would see what happens to stagnant races."

The fat man and the demon looked at each other, considering the lawyer's idea. "Yes," said the demon, puncturing his finger with the tip of his beak. "We may do just that." He allowed the black pus to drip from his finger into his beak.

Feeling warm inside, the lawyer bent to open another crate as his friends floated into different rooms. He had been alone for half an hour when he opened a crate and found an engine. A green label attached by the hawkman read "Edsel." He lifted his head to call his friends when a long shadow crept over him. "Oh. You're here," he said.

"Yeah," replied a gravelly voice, and the lawyer saw only blackness after that.

4. Something awoke the hawkman; he did not know if it was a sudden thumping or a similar noise, the dim lights shining through the open door (his bedroom was still dark), or his instincts which had been proven wrong upon so many occasions in the recent past. He had no chance to brood on the matter; for whatever reason, he was awake, *and someone was in Carter Hall.*

It seemed proper that he should be dressed before he investigated, that he should be completely within his identity. The hawkman was strangely tense; he sensed a danger which, if he had met it at some other time, at some place other than Carter Hall, he might have conquered with ease. He did not know why he felt capable of handling almost any danger; he had rarely encountered one. Nor could he explain his belief that he was about to take part in an important event. His life, if anything, had been uneventful. He wanted to think that thieves had come to Carter Hall as a prank; but although that would have been a logical explanation, he believed there was a more sinister reason. Putting on his great gray wings, he felt that the events which had suddenly been thrust upon him were beyond his control; he would act out his part like a helpless puppet; the thought made him uncomfortable.

The hawkman hesitated before lowering his mask on his head. He thought that if he wanted, he could revolt, refuse to be a puppet. He could leave Carter Hall to the thieves. But then there would have been the question of what to do next.

He lowered his mask and without another thought flew down the hall. He flew with the power of his mind rather than that of his wings; he did not want anyone to hear the rush of air or the scratching of his wings on the stone walls. As he flew, he no longer thought of himself as a puppet; whatever was happening to him was right. Perhaps he would even find his true purpose and would never be lonely again.

The hawkman flew down several stairways until he reached the second floor of the museum. Below him, in the hallway of the first floor, he heard voices.

"Who are you?" asked a gravelly voice. The voice of the godlike man with no name.

"I am the fat man."

"And I'm the demon. And *that* is our friend the lawyer lying behind you. He'll be unhappy when he wakes and finds his suit bloody."

"Never heard of you."

"That is not surprising," said the fat man, "considering the events of the recent past."

The hawkman scowled beneath his mask; he had almost forgotten *them*. He could guess what the godlike man with no name was in Carter Hall for: revenge. But the other two. . . .

"By the way, I found another of your little party sneaking around," said the godlike man with no name. "He was surprised to see me."

The fat man chuckled. "I can understand that."

"Uh, yeah. Well, listen, boys, I have some business with the hawkman to attend to, and I don't like the idea of you being here. I thought I might just send the four of you on a vacation."

The hawkman fully expected the demon and the fat man to beg for mercy, but what the demon said was:

"Don't send me to the anti-matter universe. I was there just last year."

"It is such a bore," said the fat man.

"Look at how confused he is," said the demon. "He can't understand why we're not afraid. Do you think he would be afraid of us if he could remember us?"

"Probably, but I do not see what good it would do him. Suppose we sent *him* somewhere?"

"Why waste the energy? He wants to see the hawkman, so let him see him. After we're finished."

"You are right about that, friend demon. Should we let the lawyer have a chance to deal with him?"

"I suggest we worry about that when we come to it. The lawyer's been awfully frightened about something this evening and I don't think he should be subjected to any more undue stress. Unless it's absolutely necessary, of course."

The hawkman was confused. Something at the back of his mind told him that there was indeed no reason for the demon and the fat man to worry about their antagonist. He decided that he should ignore them until later and take care of his "business" with the godlike man with no name. The hawkman walked down the stairs; he hoped that he appeared menacing and confident, in full control. On the first floor he faced the backs of the demon and the fat man.

The godlike man with no name was visibly relieved to see the hawkman. He had been standing with his legs spread, his poncho flung over his shoulder, and his hands two inches from his guns, as was his custom; but it seemed as if the godlike man with no name did not know where to go from there, as if he were searching for an excuse to retreat from the position he had selected for himself. As the hawkman walked between the demon and the fat man, shoving them to either side and then walking forward several more steps, the godlike man with no name relaxed, struck a match on the wall, lit his cigar stub, and leaned against a crate. "Your bodyguards are pretty inept," he said.

The hawkman did not answer; he was aware of the demon and the fat man whispering behind him, but he did not pay attention to what they were saying. He stared at the godlike man with no name for a moment, then said, "They're not my bodyguards; they're thieves. I'll deal with them after I deal with you."

The godlike man with no name laughed. "I just bet you will."

"I hope to do a better job dealing with them than you did."

The godlike man with no name threw his cigar on the floor. The demon and the fat man, still whispering and chuckling, floated over the pair and sat on a stack of crates. The demon pointed his finger and the unconscious lawyer floated up beside them.

"You're clever, hawkman," said the godlike man with no name. "But I won't let you get my goat."

"What other reason could you have come here for?"

"Well, about this afternoon: I realize that you were only having a little fun. I understand these things, so I was willing to let you get by with it. But, you see, it's my mule."

He paused, waiting for the implications of his words to sink into the hawkman and the audience. "He doesn't understand, not at all. He's been sulking around all day and I can't do a thing with him. I've tried explaining, but it doesn't seem to work. I was thinking that, well, maybe if you apologized . . ."

The hawkman was stunned. From nothingness he manufactured a crossbow.

The godlike man with no name continued, "Now, if you apologize, like I know you're going to, then I think I can get my mule to understand."

"And if I don't?"

The godlike man with no name shrugged and held his hands two inches from his guns.

Although they were enjoying themselves, the demon and the fat man decided that the confrontation they were watching should be more dramatic. They dimmed the museum lights and made the wind howl; the temperature dropped; outside in the blackness, litter blew across the street. The demon's penis rested on his crossed legs; the longer the antagonists faced each other, the harder he rubbed it. The fat man sat on the edge of a crate, his legs dangling, kicking back and forth; his elbows resting on his knees, his chin on his palms. He could not keep himself from smiling. "If only the lawyer were awake to see this," he whispered to the demon.

"No. He'd only ruin it by trying to get even with the old cowhand over there. It's better this way."

"Possibly, but I cannot help feeling that he would like all this. He has not had much fun recently."

"True," the demon conceded. "True."

The godlike man with no name pressed his tongue against his cheek. He had been smiling for nearly two minutes, waiting for the hawkman to raise his crossbow. "You know what I'm going to do to you?" he asked.

The hawkman scowled beneath his mask; he saw no point in answering.

"I'm going to send you and your beloved Carter Hall to the anti-matter universe. I wouldn't want you two to be separated or anything nasty like that."

"I've enough power to stop you. And to send you there instead."

"Maybe. Maybe not."

The demon leaned over and whispered to the fat man, "Those fools! Don't they realize what they're doing to us?"

The fat man pondered the matter. He pulled his white socks up from where they had fallen down annoyingly inside his spatted shoes and brushed dust from his sleeves. "Come to think of it, I do not believe they do."

"Should we stop them?"

"Already they are amassing energy. They will have to use it on something—either on us or on each other."

The demon rubbed his four nipples. "I think they should use it on each other. Let's get the lawyer and the gunsel out of here."

"A wise course of action. We must face up to the fact that we blew it very badly."

The demon, the lawyer, and the fat man disappeared, taking the hidden gunsel with them, leaving the hawkman and the godlike man with no name to finish their confrontation alone.

The godlike man with no name pulled his guns from their holsters; yellow flashes of heatless light sparkled throughout Carter Hall. The hawkman fired the arrow from the crossbow, missing his target by millimeters. The arrow punctured a crate of ancient newspapers. A rumbling sounded from the foundations of the museum. Chips of stone fell about the godlike man with no name. His arms shaking as he tried to keep his guns pointed at the hawkman, he closed his eyes and concentrated, drawing all the energy he could from the untapped power in his brain. The blood drained from his head; sweat beaded on his brow; his breath came in gasps. He staggered backward and leaned against a gray stone wall for support. But he was succeeding; Carter Hall was being whisked into the anti-matter universe.

The hawkman knew it and dropped his now useless crossbow; he fought back with equal amounts of energy. The battle quickly took its toll; he already wished he hadn't donned his mask because of the sweat dripping into his eyes. He was conscious of the sweat dripping from his hair and down his back, over his shoulders; the sweat dripping from his armpits, running down his sides. His head felt light and dizzy; his nose was clogged——he had to breathe

94

through his mouth. Once he caught a glimpse of what was going on outside the window; the blackness of night had yielded to a redness that could not be properly described as light; it was more of a glowing thin film creeping over the universe.

The hawkman and his foe, the crates surrounding them, all of Carter Hall, were tinged with the red film. The hawkman realized that if he faltered, if he allowed the godlike man with no name any more ground, then the redness, which was part of a nether region, would give way to a yellow sky dotted with black stars, and he would be lost, floating forever in the space of the anti-matter universe.

The hawkman doubted he could win; his foe had gotten a head start and the hawkman was now engaged in a holding action. Yet this doubt did not make him want to surrender; instead, he dug deeper into the resources of his brain; he would not admit defeat. He closed his eyes, clenched his fists, bent his knees, concentrated. He was the hawkman. He existed to protect Carter Hall, and he would continue to *be* the lonely hawkman.

But as the battle lengthened, the hawkman found it more and more difficult to hold his own. The walls of Carter Hall cracked——he had to divert energy to keep them whole. The more energy he diverted, the more ground he lost. He opened his eyes to see only the thinnest outline of the godlike man with no name. He shivered involuntarily as he saw the red film crawl backward and break into pieces; he saw traces of yellow and tiny black holes in space.

The hawkman found it easy to imagine what would happen back on Earth. Carter Hall would be gone as if it had never existed, and the godlike man with no name would stand there and inspect the ground where it had once rested. And he would lift his head to the night sky and laugh. He would laugh at everything—the hawkman, his heritage from the past, even the stone walls.

And the hawkman would be defeated.

The hawkman did not know how he could accept defeat.

And he would be lonelier than ever before. He would not have the limitless blue sky, the birds to talk to, nor the rippling sea to comfort him. He would have nothing but a strange new home to which he could never adjust. He could try to get back to Earth, but although there were many paths *into* the anti-matter universe, there were few back, and the hawkman doubted he could find his way home (as the demon claimed he once had). On Earth he had hope; in the anti-matter universe the hawkman could look forward to a future without hope.

Alone.

The hawkman decided that he would not be alone. Nor did he want to take a chance on finding companionship. (Other godlike men had been sent to the anti-matter universe, but it was so vast that the possibilities of discovering someone else were almost nonexistent.) The hawkman was near exhaustion. He ran his tongue over his upper lip and tasted his salty sweat. If he was to act, if he was to find a friend, he had to act soon, while he still had the strength.

He stopped fighting back. The redness suddenly disappeared, and there was only the yellow and the black. But the thin outline of the godlike man with no name lingered, and before it faded, the hawkman reached out and seized his opponent.

He sank to his knees, leaning against a crate containing part of his heritage. He felt his nemesis rushing toward him.

He had not been defeated after all.

5. The demon cleaned his hand with his tongue. "I'm glad we didn't have to fight the hawkman. Did you see the godlike man with no name disappear? A neat trick, as they say."

The fat man sidestepped a board lying on the golden sidewalk. "Too bad we had to send the lawyer and the gunsel back to their apartment. They would have enjoyed it immensely." He watched the clouds cover the moon. "Hmmm. It might rain."

"Good," said the demon. "It'll wash some of the dirt away."

The fat man mumbled an answer and they made their way home in silence until the fat man said, "Do you feel a sense of loss?"

The demon pondered the question. "Now that you mention it, yes. I might never have noticed it if you hadn't brought it up."

"Imagine, the joke is on us!" said the fat man, restraining himself from laughing. "All these eons and we did not care for our past, and now that Carter Hall is gone, we miss it!" His mood became more somber. "I wonder why."

"Perhaps because we knew that while it was there we could find the answers if we really wanted them. Now if we should need them—well, they're gone."

The fat man rubbed his chin. "Yes. That might be it. Indeed, that might be it."

Again, they were silent; they were very tired and wanted to sleep.

SLICES OF LIFE: THREE

The middleman sensed his life had once been dangerous; he sensed he had once been a totally independent individual who would harm a friend for the good of the state or
who would harm the state for the good of a friend, depending on which was more important to him at the moment.
He believed that once, instead of being a middleman, he
had been a man in the middle. The forces of good and evil
had always tried to sway him; and he had laughed because
he needed neither one. As the middleman slept in his small
bachelor apartment, he dreamed of stumbling across mur-
dered bodies among the garbage cans in alleys or among
the scattered groceries lying on the kitchen floor; and of
pulling a gun from a shoulder holster and firing bullets at a
fleeing target; and of spying on a beautiful woman and
knowing that he could seduce her easily, without half-
trying, just by the way she looked at him. He dreamed of a
life full of unexpected dangers, startling coincidences, utter
good fortune, and unforgettable surprises; he dreamed of
never knowing what was going to happen next and of taking joy in that fact; he dreamed of living through eternity
with a gusto he could not summon as a middleman.

Sitting up in his moderately comfortable bed with light
blue blankets which he said kept him "lukewarm," he
rubbed his large green eyes. He yawned. His mouth felt dry
and sticky; he imagined yellow stains on his teeth that
would never brush off. He was a godlike man of medium

height, with smooth muscles rippling under his tanned, slender arms and chest; with pale lanky legs; and with a thin, haggard face that made him appear to be alert and in full control, but a face that seemed as if its owner were about to degenerate into absent-mindedness at any moment.

The middleman walked to the bathroom, relieved himself, washed his hands, and looked at himself in the mirror. He realized that he was ugly. He had once been astonishingly handsome.

He brushed his teeth, combed his short blond hair, shaved, and pulled out four ingrown hairs. He did thirty push-ups, fifty-seven correct sit-ups, and three incorrect sit-ups. He changed boxer shorts and dressed in black socks, brown trousers, a white shirt, a black tie, and a brown jacket. He examined himself in the mirror over the dresser. He was still ugly, but at least he looked honest.

He vaguely recalled a day when he had not looked so honest. He had looked evil. The forces of good had always been after him. But he had lived by his wits, by quick thinking, and by the favors of those nice perverts who wanted to see the bad guy win, no matter what he had done. The middleman sensed that he had committed unforgivable crimes, terrible, foul, unspeakable crimes; but he felt no remorse. He felt proud. He had threatened helpless old women. He had spit upon the sidewalk. He had taken marbles from children in a rigged game. He had torn dolls apart. He had robbed the bank. He had manipulated the stock market. He had committed breach of promise twelve times, and he had loved it every time. He had dealt from the bottom of the deck. He had deliberately called the pitch a ball when it had been a strike.

However, he had faith. He would be evil again; he would experience every sensation to its utmost; life would indeed by a collection of moments upon moments, instead of the lengthy, drab, monotonous singular moment it now was. The middleman held firm to the belief that life repeated itself, that life formed itself along patterns, even as godlike men patterned their lives. Therefore, it stood to reason that the middleman would again be evil.

Boy, he thought, *ain't life circular?*

Then he experienced another moment of doubt. Perhaps

he was only deluding himself. Perhaps life was not circular after all.

Since he was never sure of anything in the morning, the middleman decided to go to his office at the North Pole and work.

He teleported himself to his secretary's office.

"Morning, Zelda. That's a real nice trench coat you have there. I dig red."

Popping her chewing gum, Zelda, a pig from the North Pole, said, "Thank you. And good morning to you, boss middleman." She walked to the coffee pot in the corner of her tiny office and poured herself a cup, tossing in two lumps of sugar. The office furniture was functional and plain; the chairs were black leather; the rugs were red and they slid across the wooden floor if someone was not careful when he walked over them. The wooden, wobbly desk was covered with candy snacks, wrappers, pencils, pens, and stacks of paper. The middleman did not see the typewriter. "Do you want a cup of coffee, sir?" asked Zelda, smoothing her trench coat behind her legs and sitting down. The middleman lost sight of her; she was totally hidden by her paperwork.

"No. What's on the schedule today, dearie?"

"Oh, I just love it when you call me that, boss middleman. Ooh! Well, nothing to speak of. Just the usual rigamarole. And the tap-dancing locust have got into the corn again."

"Yeah. I heard. We'll have to do something about that, but I don't know just what. I'd hate to have to send them to the anti-matter universe. Anything else?"

Zelda cleared her throat. "There is *one* problem. I hope you won't be angry at me, sir."

"Not a chance, toots. What's the problem? Well, come on and spit it out. You know I can handle almost anything. Usually I handle it right proper too."

"It's Shadwell, sir. He rushed into your office and he won't come out. I tried to get rid of him, sir."

"Don't let it get to you, kid. You did your best. I'll take care of it."

The middleman unbuttoned his jacket, put his right hand into his pocket, stuck out his left hand, walked to the door of his office, turned the doorknob, and strode inside. He

101

strode with confidence: Shadwell was only a yellow pig with a corkscrew tail and a trench coat, no match for a godlike man.

The middleman's office was far from functional. It had three couches, two of which folded out into beds. There were four bookshelves devoted to the great works of god-like mankind, by such undeniable geniuses as the portly author, the Southern gentleman, the poet who yearned for the return of childhood and, most important of all, the complete output of the Big Red Cheese. The middleman's quartz desk was ten yards long, five yards wide; on top of it was an inkwell and a quill pen; the high-backed chair behind the desk glistened in the sunlight and glowed in the dark. The green rug was so soft that when business was slow, the middleman leaped over his desk and hit the floor not with a thud, but with a puff; the middleman then rolled about like an eternal child playing in the grass.

Enigmatic paintings that people always explained to the middleman hung on the blue walls; the middleman could never remember the explanations.

Through his picture window the middleman could see the fields tended by the pigs, and he was always satisfied to know that everything was going well.

Shadwell sat in an easy chair. He smoked one of the middleman's choice cigars and rested his bare feet on the quartz desk. Shadwell was smaller than most yellow pigs; he was slimmer because he jogged five kilometers every morning. His stubby snout was acutely sensitive to odors and his black eyes looked like glass. He was naked; his trench coat was crumpled in a corner.

The middleman stiffened when he noticed Shadwell's nudity. Shadwell always bothered him. If Shadwell could not get what he considered important, then he made up for it in little ways, usually at the expense of the middleman's pride. Shadwell was definitely an uppity yellow pig.

"Well, fancy meeting you here, Shadwell. How goes it?" The middleman smiled so wide his face hurt. It always hurt his face when he smiled at Shadwell.

"You know how it goes, boscoe," said Shadwell, blowing a smoke ring and avoiding the middleman's stare. "I'm not getting any younger."

"Neither am I."

"But you aren't getting any older, either."

The middleman tapped his toe. He pursed his lips. He knew that when he pursed his lips he was not ugly, but *ugly*! The middleman felt he had spent most of his life waiting for Shadwell to die, although he had spent but a few years. He was tempted to see personally to Shadwell's demise.

"Listen, Shadwell, I'd love to mess around with you, but I have orders to fill. I have to send corn all over Earth today! Corn and carrots and squash. . . ."

"Squash! Ecch!"

"Especially squash. And tomatoes and beans! There's a lot of crops out here at the North Pole and it's my job to get it to the people. A civilization depends on me. People don't waste their energy on something as trivial as food! And that's why I can't fool around with you. Understand?"

Shadwell leaped from the easy chair and paced circles around the middleman. The middleman increased his body odor to annoy Shadwell, but the pig was so agitated that he ignored the smell. "Then you should be able to understand my problem," said Shadwell, holding his hands behind his back. "I'm just an insignificant pig. I want to do something *important*. You can give me power and fame and glory. You can give me a direction in life. You can do it easily. You should understand because here you are, wasting your time at the North Pole doing something anybody could do. You have all eternity before you and you aren't doing something important! We're in the same boat, boscoe!"

The middleman sighed. He knew that he would not be able to stomach Shadwell any longer. "Shadwell, my dear pig, I hate to do this, but I really ain't got no choice."

Shadwell stopped pacing and opened his mouth to speak; he knew what the middleman was about to do. But the middleman did it before Shadwell had an opportunity to protest.

The middleman sent the pig to a cornfield thirty kilometers away.

"If nothing else, that oughta keep him out of my hair for a while." The middleman sat behind his desk and relaxed. He could not summon the necessary sense of purpose to begin work. And he had told Shadwell the truth. The race of godlike men needed food. He had a lot of work to do.

His mind wandered. It seemed that his mind wandered more and more recently. He would never admit it to Shadwell, but he understood the need for fame and glory. The middleman sensed that once his life had been the most marvelous of all, greater and more significant than even the life of the Big Red Cheese. He had commanded respect; not even the eternal children 'had poked fun at him. He had once dressed with flair; his colorful clothes had been outrageous, but tasteful; they invariably became the lastest fashion fad. People had come to him and asked his opinion about certain matters, usually public matters, but sometimes private, deeply personal matters. He had answered them with discretion and wit, realizing that the people 'had cared not so much for his opinion on public or private matters, but had cared instead for his approval of *them*. He had always given them encouragement; he had told them that they should continue what they were doing if they believed in it, even if he disapproved of them. He had been aware of his grave responsibility.

He wondered what had been the reason for his fall from grace. He tried to think back, to recall more details; he could not.

He did know that the time would come when he would no longer be needed at the North Pole; his life would once again be glorious. The knowledge was all that sustained him through the day.

Gee, I sure do hope life is circular, he thought.

CHAPTER FOUR

1. The night after the lonely hawkman and Carter Hall had been sent to the anti-matter universe, an unusual number of godlike men woke early. Inexplicably distressed and confused, they needed their sleep; but they were too uncomfortable to close their eyes and wrap themselves tighter in their blankets. Even though the curtains were drawn, they imagined the sun shining in their eyes. They got out of bed, brushed their teeth, dressed, had a drink of orange juice, and wandered about with no particular destination in mind. They were not depressed; they merely felt duty-bound to ponder philosophical questions they could not articulate.

The unusual number was not large. Nearly two hundred found themselves wandering toward the site of Carter Hall.

The bright young aristocrat who was a serf to his valet said, "It's . . . it's . . . it's. . . ."

The valet said, "Gone, I fancy, is the word you are groping for, sir."

"Yes, thank you. It's gone as if it had never existed."

"An original, succinct phrase, sir."

"Thank you. I don't know what I would do without you."

The aristocrat and his valet, like so many others, said little else and walked about the ruins of the apartment complexes, hoping to find some forgotten fragment of Carter Hall. They found nothing.

The poet who yearned for the return of his youth wondered if he had, indeed, lost it a second time. "It would be sad if my youth had been here all along," he said pompously, "and I just didn't know it." When he discovered that no one was listening, he left in a huff.

The little lady with a quick, personal wit and bandages on her wrists said, "Maybe I'll try again. My bathtub is clean and my razor blades are sharp. Then when I'm well this afternoon, everything will be hunkey-dory."

The thin man forgot all about his traps for the snapping turtles.

The centaur pranced about, listening to his hooves clomp on the golden concrete. He kicked a rock to the other side of the street and watched it roll to a stop.

The priest decided that he should wait a few days before writing another fairy tale. The eternal children never paid attention, anyway.

Two whacky, lovable gangsters who had celebrated their honeymoon by knocking over a bank also wandered about, their pug-faced right-hand man behind them. Occasionally, they opened their violin cases to see if their machine guns were loaded. They glanced to their sides to see if the fat Southern cop ("Well, we got you dis time, boy!") was behind them. They laughed at the confusion and sadness of their fellows, sent their right-hand man off to create some bullets, and made love on a blanket, eating fried chicken afterward.

No one saw the gunsel, but he was there. He had not been told that the godlike man with no name had been taken to the anti-matter universe, and he wanted revenge. He soon saw that there was no hope of revenge, and he realized that the people were feeling a sense of loss that might, *just might* make them depressed. He reported his findings to the fat man.

Upon hearing his report, the fat man and the demon forgot all about their lack of sleep. They rushed to the lawyer's apartment and told him the good news. The lawyer forgot all about his terrific headache and the bottle of aspirin he was swallowing. They rushed to the site of Carter Hall. They were noticed by several godlike men, but no one cared to remember who they were. They did not mind; they were concerned with other things.

The demon jabbed the lawyer twice in the side, almost

106

knocking the lawyer over. "Watch! Watch! Don't take your eyes off this scene for a second! Sweet victory is within our grasp!"

The fat man rested his hands on his great bulk and said, "Look at them moping around. Once again a report from my gunsel has proved to be perfectly accurate. I must confess, for a moment I was doubtful. But I am satisifed; my faith has been justified."

The lawyer grimaced and stepped away from the demon when his friend tried to jab him a third time. "Too bad we had nothing to do with it."

The fat man's jaw dropped; he caught saliva with his hand before it landed on his clean white suit. He sent the saliva and (through an error of judgment) a slice of epidermis to the anti-matter universe. "Friend lawyer! What do you mean? We were there, were we not? We were hot on the trail of depression! Say that we were, and I will allow you to sit in the Morris chair all you want!"

The lawyer could not bear to see the fat man quiver in frustration; he turned away and looked at the centaur prance about as he said, "As a lawyer, I'm supposed to know these things. You told me the godlike man with no name sent Carter Hall away. *That* has made these people sad. We may have been hot on the trail, but the trail was whisked away."

They were silent. Although he was obsessed by the thought of failure, the lawyer searched for a glimpse of Kitty. The demon drank blood from his finger.

Finally the fat man snorted. "Disgusting! Are you trying to take away our victory? I am surprised at you. You have worked almost as hard as the demon and I."

"Just as hard," said the lawyer, shaking his fist.

"He may be right," said the demon. "We did nothing. If these people become depressed, we can't take the credit for it."

"We may swindle, cheat, steal, and be altogether nasty blokes," said the lawyer, "but we must be honest. If we claim that the loss of Carter Hall is our handiwork, and if the truth is discovered, then we'll be back where we started. Worse, maybe."

The fat man visibly brought himself under control. He withdrew a white handkerchief from his coat pocket and wiped his brow. His breathing was heavy and his face was red. "Forgive me," he implored. "It was unseemly of me to lose my grasp on reality. It was just that we were so close to success. So close."

The demon slapped his forehead; he had had a sudden revelation. His friends stared at him; he stared back.

The fat man said, "Well? What is it?"

"What if these fools get depressed and we've had nothing to do with it?" asked the demon, accidently squeezing his penis too hard. *"Then* where will we be?"

The lawyer, forgetting all about Kitty, said, "We'll have lost all our fame and glory for nothing!" His eyes darted about madly. "We'll have nothing to sustain us through our own, uh, depression."

"I was afraid you'd say that," murmured the demon.

"Then there is only one thing we can do," said the fat man.

The lawyer jumped up and down. "Quick! Quick! Tell us before it's too late!"

"We must make these godlike men happy."

"Make them happy?" asked the lawyer, almost dropping his sword-cane. "Make them happy? Why, that's contrary to everything we've ever stood for!" To illustrate his point, the lawyer kicked at a rock, and missed. His derby rolled from his head and he inadvertently stepped on it. "How can you say that? How can we just turn around, after all our hard work to push these nerds over the precipice of despair, and make them happy?" He mentally repaired his derby and placed it on his head.

The fat man answered calmly, "We have no choice. The return of depression must be *our* doing, no matter what the cost. Mere ideals have no place in affairs of this order."

The lawyer knew the fat man was never wrong when he was in control of himself, so he said, "All right, we'll make them happy. But how?"

"Know any good jokes?" asked the demon.

Silence was his answer.

The demon picked his lower right nostril and said, "Now that I think of it, we aren't much when it comes to one-liners. Perhaps some slapstick will do."

"I do not mind," said the fat man, brushing dust from his

white jacket, "as long as I do not have to roll around in the dirt."

"I don't like pain," said the lawyer. "Just as long as I don't get hurt."

"And I'm too dignified for that sort of thing," said the demon. "So I guess it takes care of that idea."

Before the demon could bring up the subject of absurd humor, the fat man clapped his hands and said, "Over there is the galactic hero with two right arms. He is our man."

"Him?" asked the lawyer.

"I have had dealings with him before. Watch. Then do as I do." He smiled enigmatically.

The galactic hero with two right arms was marching over the former boundaries of Carter Hall. The many bronze and silver medals completely covering his chest jingled with each goose step. He did not alter his eyes-front position. His boyish, clean-shaven face tried to assume the appearance of a savage, cold soldier, but the thin, trembling lines of his mouth hinted that the galactic hero was close to tears. Not only was he, in his own way, inspecting the site and searching for a trace of the building, but he was bestowing upon it the highest honor he could give: marching back and forth as if he were guarding something precious. Many godlike men noted this, even the lovers/gangsters eating fried chicken, and they nodded in approval, tears in their eyes.

The fat man chuckled to himself as if he had just coaxed the lawyer out of the Morris chair. He watched the scene with his arms crossed and with his foot tapping to the silent rhythm of the march. He tilted his head several times to the right and the left, waiting for the perfect moment to proceed with his plan to make the godlike men happy. Then, without warning, to the amazement of his two friends, he marched in goose step toward the galactic hero and fell in behind him. His fat cheeks and his tremendous belly bounced up and down; during the moments when he stood on one leg, he swayed back and forth with the breeze. Once he almost lost his balance and toppled over, but he righted himself without losing a step.

The demon and the lawyer looked at each other in confusion. The demon rolled his eyes to the sky; the lawyer licked his upper lip. "He wants us to do that?" asked the lawyer.

"He wants us to do that," said the demon.

They shrugged. The lawyer sent his sword-cane to his apartment and marched. The demon floated beside him, swinging his arms in cadence. They fell in beside the fat man; they felt silly and embarassed, but no sacrifice was too great if it would make the onlookers happy.

Several godlike men forgot all about the loss of Carter Hall as they saw the three unknowns march. They pointed at them and made disparaging remarks. They jabbed their friends in the side and snickered. The lovers/gangsters dropped their fried chicken in surprise. The three marching friends smiled in satisfaction. And the galactic hero, the object of the joke, seemed not to notice.

Suddenly the galactic hero halted. His two right arms snapped into a salute. The fat man, not hesitating for an instant, did likewise. The demon and the lawyer looked at each other in confusion, shrugged, and saluted.

Someone guffawed. Upon reflecting back on the incident, the demon, the lawyer, and the fat man were unable to remember exactly who it had been; they would have liked to congratulate him for his impeccable taste. They finally decided that only what had happened next was the important thing: gradually everyone was guffawing. Godlike men rolled on the ground, slamming their fists on the concrete, sending chips flying into the air. Others sat down with their arms folded across their stomachs and with their eyes closed; they wanted to stop guffawing, but could not. Others stood leaning backward, their hands on their bellies. And others looked in amazement at their friends, laughing with them, mutually approving the three peculiar geniuses who had saved them from the curse of verging on depression.

The galactic hero did not seem to notice the guffawing. His face was not red with anger and he was still saluting. The lawyer whispered, "He must have an overblown sense of honor."

The demon said, "Yes, he does. And so do we for keeping this up longer than we have to. I want to go back to my apartment and rest my arms."

"An excellent suggestion," said the fat man.

All at once the trio snapped their arms to their sides, did an about-face, and marched twenty meters away from the galactic hero, where they fell out of formation. The people gave them a standing ovation. The lawyer, his sword-cane suddenly appearing in one hand, took off his derby and bowed. "Thank you, thank you, my friends," he said.

The fat man stuffed his hands in his pockets and nodded at the people in appreciation. "The best is yet to come," he said.

"Indeed," said the demon. "When we're through every guffaw, aye, every chuckle will be more important than ever before."

Someone yelled, "Author! Author!"

The fat man waved to the crowd. "I must take the credit for the little drama which has just unfolded before your eyes. But I must also thank my two friends, the demon and the lawyer, for their support was needed to make the drama the smashing success that it was."

The people cheered and cheered.

2. The other fat man breathed deeply; the odor of his greenhouse full of black orchids brightened his spirits considerably. He allowed himself to smile; no one was watching, so it could not possibly do any harm to his image. He was not the type to act eccentrically most of the time and then suddenly act like any normal godlike man for the slightest reason, not even because of the pleasure his orchids gave him. The fact that only two other godlike men —the cook and the witty leg man—knew that he was eccentric did not bother him. He was top dog, and he knew it; there was no reason why anyone else should.

At least, there had been no reason until rather peculiar events had occurred which had changed the carefully built pattern of his life.

Despite the fact that he was larger than the fat man, the other fat man moved with more grace and ease. He was fond of telling his employees that had he wished, he could have been the ballet dancer. (The witty leg man always made some snide remark whenever he heard this confes-

111

sion, but even he had to admit that his boss was far from being clumsy.) The other fat man plucked a black orchid, sniffed it, glanced upward at the sunlight shining through the glass roof, and ran the stem through the lapel of his brown jacket. Although it was time for him to leave the greenhouse and pursue his other habits, he was reluctant to leave because he wanted to gloat over how satisfactory his orchids were doing and because this most private area of his ivory tower lulled his anxieties. It had been many eons since he had had to take overt action—or even send his witty leg man to take overt action—and he was uncomfortably afraid that he was out of practice.

He slowly walked the paths of the greenhouse. He saw only the black orchids flicking in and out of his sight. It was difficult for him to blank his mind of all important thought and to concentrate on his insignificant pleasures. The orchids had been his one concern for eons; and for eons he had worked so that they would be his one concern. He knew that except for one quality he was no different than any other godlike man, despite his well-cultivated eccentricities; and that quality was genius. Genius used to influence others, to make them bend, unknowingly, to his will. Genius used to insure that facet of his existence which was most precious to him—his own peace and quiet.

His mouth twisted out of line a little. He glanced again at the sky; he was surprised at himself. If he was no longer able to control himself when he was alone, how would he act in the presence of others?

He had no way of knowing. He could only proceed as if nothing was at stake, as if he was simply asking a favor (which was his method of demanding).

To divert himself from his self-doubts, he wondered about what his cook should fix for dinner. Something fattening, he decided. It was always better to put on weight naturally rather than with the powers of his mind. Something rare. Something exquisite. Perhaps lamb kidneys served mountain-style with dumplings and brown sugar. Perhaps trout Montbarry, with parsley, onions, chives, chervil, tarragon, fresh mushrooms, brandy, bread crumbs, fresh eggs, paprika, tomatoes, and cheese. Perhaps a four-month old cockerel trained to eat blueberries from infancy, cooked with mushrooms, tarragon, and white wine. Or perhaps something even more interesting. Of course, the cook would create the ingredients from his own mind; none of that stuff grown by the yellow pigs in the trench coats was good enough for the other fat man.

He sighed. He needed a beer. But he did not want to drink one just yet because it would lead, he knew, to another. Although he could drink several bottles and not feel the alcohol, his bladder was weak and sometimes he had to urinate every thirty minutes for several hours, and that was if he held himself back as long as possible. He did not care to think what would happen to his conference if he had to leave every thirty minutes to urinate. Its effectiveness would surely be diminished.

He sighed again. He realized that no matter what, he would have to leave the greenhouse soon. It was almost time to change from his canary yellow shirt into another canary yellow shirt. Never before had the thought of performing this custom irritated him; this was indeed strange. He wondered if his life would change regardless of what he tried to do about it.

At least he did not have to worry about the witty leg man; there was one godlike man who could take care of himself in any situation. If the other fat man was sure of anything, it was that the witty leg man, despite the fact that he was in name a hireling, was his friend and would stand by him. The other fat man smiled to himself again, this time not worried about showing his emotions. For some reason he was not ashamed of depending on someone. He was still afraid as he got on the elevator and descended to the ground floor where his office was; but there was also an odd warm feeling in his stomach that was vaguely comforting.

3. After they had left the former site of Carter Hall, the demon, the lawyer, and the fat man took a morning stroll that lasted long into the afternoon. The sun was covered by black clouds; it was one of those days when rain was imminent, but never came. The lawyer felt that he should be depressed, considering that it was such a dreary day for a walk; but he was not depressed; he was too busy basking in a touch of fame and glory. True, it was not the level of approbation he had known; people still ignored him. However, it was better than nothing.

The demon and the fat man felt the same way. They, too, were proud that the word about their little drama had spread fast, that the race of godlike man was learning that they should not be ignored because of their most original minds and their keen sense of humor.

The trio waved at eternal children pointing at them. People leaned out of their apartment windows and gawked, calling their spouses to take a look at them. The dogs did not bark at them, but came over and sniffed at their trouser cuffs (or at the demon's penis). The fat man was particularly fond of taking off his Borsalino and bowing; he had not realized how much he had missed fame and glory; he no longer believed that he had to some extent adjusted to his impoverished state.

"Fickle, aren't they?" asked the lawyer, tipping his black derby at a very lovely godlike woman.

"You can say that again," said the demon, "but please don't."

The fat man exclaimed something about the profits of exercise; he had totally forgotten about their last long walk through the golden apartment complexes with the golden gutters. He complimented everyone, even the most bothersome dirty eternal children who demanded in whiny voices that he tell them all about himself. He walked with his white jacket unbuttoned and with his thumbs hooked in his white suspenders, taking the longest, lankiest steps he could. His smile never faltered.

However, neither did his devotion to his purpose falter; not for a moment did he consider forgetting all about depression and taking the tried and true paths to greater fame and glory. He knew that the demon was also remaining faithful to their cause. But when the lawyer mumbled, "I wonder if Kitty has seen me yet," the fat man knew that it might be difficult for the lawyer to continue making the sacrifices necessary for their goal to be achieved.

The fat man said, "If Kitty has seen you, then she most assuredly is unimpressed."

The lawyer turned red and said, "Now just what do you mean?"

"If she had been impressed, she would have run outside and talked to you, like everyone else."

"Kitty isn't *like* everybody else," said the lawyer, twirling his sword-cane, glad that he had lost his heart to an unusual godlike woman.

"You're correct," said the demon, who had realized what the fat man was doing. "It takes a lot more than a little drama to impress her."

"Something grandiose; something unheard of!" said the fat man.

The lawyer frowned for the first time during their stroll. "You're both right. Not until everyone is hopelessly depressed will I stand a chance with her." He was silent for a moment. "I wonder if that unfaithful wench is still seeing the Big Red Cheese. I've a good mind to sic the tiny green worm on him."

"You don't want to do that," said the demon. "That nefarious creature doesn't have a mind of his own. And all you have to do to get rid of him is to smash his glasses."

The lawyer nodded in agreement; he patted an eternal child on the head and removed his hand from the vicinity of the brat's mouth just in time. "After this is over, if the Big Red Cheese is still molesting her, then I'll ask the gunsel to shadow him. That ought to be the perfect punishment for taking advantage of her."

The demon and the fat man congratulated the lawyer for his presence of mind. Now they were sure that he would not stray from the proper path.

Suddenly the fat man shortened his long and jaunty steps; he buttoned his jacket. The demon and the lawyer were too busy waving to their fans to notice. The fat man scowled; he felt nervous, and that could mean only one thing: someone was shadowing *him*. Rubbing his chin, he scrutinized the people surrounding him. He recognized everyone; the mysterious giant foot, the quivering gentleman with blinders around his eyes joyfully complaining about sensory overloads, the ape man swinging from golden gutter to golden gutter, and all the rest. He deliberately dropped his Borsalino and kicked it backward with his foot, so he would have to turn around to pick it up. This maneu-

115

ver accomplished, he saw one godlike man new to him.

The godlike man was the witty leg man, who was no fool; he saw through the fat man's ruse. He picked his flat nose to see what the fat man's reaction would be. He smiled when the fat man smiled at him. He wore a dark blue suit with a light blue shirt and tan tie. He tipped his Panama hat as the fat man put his Borsalino on his head. He leaned against a golden apartment building; he did not look particularly menacing, but that was not his job. He blew cigarette smoke in the manner of one who likes to watch it swirl until it disappears in the air, but he did not take his eyes off the three friends. The fat man quickly noted that he was handsome, healthy, and very possibly graceful; if he was indeed a foe, then he was one to be reckoned with.

The witty leg man walked toward the trio. The fat man plucked at the lawyer's sleeve and nodded toward the witty leg man. The demon wondered what was going on and turned around. Before the witty leg man was within speaking distance, they told the eternal children to leave because privacy was necessary. The eternal children did not want to go, but scampered when the demon told them he would turn them into frogs. The godlike men and women leaning out of their apartment windows turned away because they realized something was afoot, and they would learn about it soon enough when someone was claiming more fame and glory.

"I was wondering when you would notice me," said the witty leg man. "A lot of lovely godlike women already have."

"Are you making a slam at Kitty, you pig?" said the lawyer. "If you are, you'll soon know better!"

The witty leg man laughed and flicked his cigarette— which he had smoked to the butt—into a puddle. "No. I've heard of Kitty, but I've never seen her. I just meant that I've made no attempts to hide from you." He grinned. "I'm too forward for things like that."

The lawyer muttered, "Does he mean that he's been forward with Kitty? Does he? Does he?"

The demon licked the left side of his beak. "No. He's too forward to be forward behind someone's back."

The lawyer held his fist in front of the fat man's mouth.

116

"Where's the gunsel? Why didn't he send this nit to the anti-matter universe?"

The fat man made the noise he always made when he was about to spit; the lawyer put his fist under his left arm-pit. "Did I not tell you?" asked the fat man. "I sent the gunsel home. His bunions were hurting him."

The lawyer did not know what to say. His mouth dropped open and swung up and down; he stuttered a few phrases. He walked in a circle, held his sword-cane above his head, stopped, lowered his sword-cane, and finally was able to articulate, "Bunions! Bunions! The gunsel has bunions?"

"And flat feet, too," said the fat man. "Do not let the word get around; my gunsel thinks that it would mar his image as an instrument of terror."

"Of course, he doesn't have much of an image now," said the witty leg man.

"What do you mean he hasn't got an image?" asked the lawyer. "Of course he has an image! Everybody's afraid of him! Even me—oops." The lawyer pursed his mouth. He did not want to talk again for a long time.

"I meant that he's not as well-known as he used to be," said the witty leg man, lighting a cigarette.

The lawyer forgot his desire to keep quiet. "Even though people don't know who he is, they're still afraid of him!"

"More or less," replied the witty leg man, shrugging.

The lawyer raised his finger, meaning to say something else, something that would humble this stranger. When he could think of nothing damaging enough, he merely glared, turned away, and tapped his foot.

The demon also raised a finger at the witty leg man. A dead fly hung from his fingernail. "I assume that you've some business with us. If so, what is it?"

"I don't have business with you; my employer does. I've just been sent to get you."

"Oh?" said the fat man. "And who is this employer?"

"You wouldn't know."

The lawyer stamped his foot, a bit too hard; he winced from the pain. "Is he implying that we're dumb? Does he think we're stupid? Does he think he can intimidate a keen intellect like mine?"

The witty leg man pretended not to have heard the lawyer. "My employer is not known to you. Unlike you three, however, his anonymity wasn't thrust upon him; he just prefers it that way."

The lawyer whistled. "He must be weird."

"Practical would be a better word," said the witty leg man. "He's also unfathomable, mysterious, ever-changing, omniscient, and omnipresent."

"Only one man could possibly fulfill those qualifications," said the lawyer.

"Then you know who he is?" exclaimed the witty leg man. "That's impossible!"

"I don't know who he is," said the lawyer. "I figured it was impossible for two people to be stupid enough to deliberately take on such pointless traits."

The fat man laughed and applauded; he said again and again, "Oh, that was pretty good. Completely unexpected!" The demon chuckled and patted the lawyer on the head. The lawyer blushed and said, "Aw, it was nothing."

When the fat man finally stopped laughing he said, "This is all very interesting, but some day we must get to the grit of the matter. What business does your employer have with us?"

"He wants to talk to you."

"What's in it for us?" asked the demon.

The witty leg man smiled. "More than you have ever dreamed, if you cooperate." He gestured at the golden apartment buildings surrounding them. "You see, he simply runs the whole show."

The lawyer's mouth dropped open. The demon removed his hand from his penis and rubbed the tip of his beak. The fat man drummed his fingers on his vast stomach. For the first time all three of them were speechless at once.

"Although it might come as a surprise to you, one with absolute power doesn't need to be conceited," continued the witty leg man. "So my employer doesn't even have an original name; he calls himself the other fat man."

The fat man frowned in thought and nodded. "An excellent choice; I approve." He had recovered from his initial shock; in fact, he was intrigued. Turning to his friends, he said, "Do you think we should visit this other fat man? I think it would be quite to our advantage."

The demon and the lawyer consented. Then the lawyer

118

pressed the button of his sword-cane and nicked his finger on the blade; his face was grim as he said, "Do you think this planet is big enough for two fat men?"

The fat man replied, "Earth was big enough before we gained this knowledge; whether or not it will remain so depends on this other fat man."

4. The demon, the lawyer, and the fat man peered at the clouds; they were looking for the top of the ivory tower. "So this is where the world is governed," said the fat man. "Who would have thought of an ivory tower?"

The witty leg man grinned. "My employer has subtle ways of making sure that few notice it and that none are curious."

Trying to glare at the witty leg man, the lawyer sneezed because he was allergic to the black orchids surrounding the tower. "That's a very curious statement," he said

"Thank you. It's just one of my many methods of luring the unsuspecting inside."

The lawyer immediately had visions of his body being shredded by huge and rusty machines, of a life spent as a door-to-door cheese-straightener salesman, of a world without Kitty. He wanted to shake in fright, but would not allow himself. Once again he did not want his friends to know that he was capable of fear. He took off his derby and wiped sweat from his forehead. He turned away from the ivory tower, toward the fields of black orchids. He sneezed. After wiping his nose with a handkerchief, he sent the tainted silk to the laundry bag inside his apartment. "Don't you think the gunsel should be here too?" he asked the fat man.

Sniffing a black orchid (which he had not picked up by bending over, but by making the flower tear itself from the ground and float up to him), the fat man said, "No. What is there to fear?"

The witty leg man grinned. The lawyer did not like the grin, but when he saw the fat man grinning back the same way, he decided there was nothing he could do about it. He turned to the demon, who was also sniffing a black orchid. "Don't you think we need the gunsel?"

"Certainly not for protection," said the demon. "He hasn't been doing too well in that department lately." The demon crumpled the orchid and rubbed it over his hands. "I like these orchids," he said to the lawyer. "They remind me of green bedspreads, and you know what my green bedspreads remind me of."

"Your brothers," answered the lawyer.

The demon snorted; the fat man pretended not to have heard; neither wanted to think of the sordid incident concerning the demon's nine brothers that had occurred several eons ago. Wondering what the lawyer had been talking about, the witty leg man rang the doorbell three times—two shorts and a long. "I imagine you want to get this over with," he said.

"Not really," said the fat man. "I find this experience fascinating." He paused, then added, "So far."

They heard the sounds of locks clicking and scraping. The lawyer wished that he had thought to count them; there must have been at least twenty. The cook opened the door and ushered them in. The witty leg man said to the cook, "I trust the old man knows we're here."

Before the cook could answer, a voice spoke from the office. "Pfui. I am not the old man. I am the other fat man. See that you remember that in the future."

"I'll do my best," said the witty leg man. He offered to take the fat man's Borsalino and the lawyer's derby and hang them on the walnut rack; he shrugged when his offer was refused.

Fondling his penis, the demon looked over the rubber-tiled hallway. He searched for splinters on the bench, a crack in the huge mirror, the umbrella he had lost a century ago. He glanced into the front room, searching for a missing piece on the checkerboard, a scratch on the piano, ashes in the fireplace, or dirt on the yellow walls. He gave up, deciding that such picky activities were better suited to the personality of the lawyer.

The witty leg man led them to the office. The lawyer blinked and squinted; eight powerful lamps had been switched on.

The other fat man sat behind an uncluttered cherrywood

desk; the lawyer felt there should have been many items on it. Approximately twelve hundred titles had been crammed into the bookshelves; the works of the Big Red Cheese were conspicuous by their absence. Where there were no bookshelves, the other fat man had hung outdated maps. A huge globe of the Earth as it presently looked stood between two red leather chairs facing the cherrywood desk. Small yellow straightback chairs were scattered throughout the room.

The witty leg man sat down on the swivel chair next to his personal desk.

Suddenly the lawyer tripped over the edge of the yellow rug and stumbled toward the other fat man's desk. The other fat man looked peeved, and the lawyer realized that he had made some sort of social blunder. Trying to take everyone's mind off his clumsiness, he blurted, "What? No Morris chairs? This is disgusting!" He turned toward the demon and the fat man. "I don't think we should stay another instant in such a barbaric room!"

"You may leave if you want," said the other fat man, evidently undisturbed by the lawyer's remarks, "because I am not holding you here. But I might add that should you decide to stay, you should conduct yourself like a gentleman."

The lawyer looked to the fat man for moral support; he received none; the fat man was too busy sizing up the other fat man. The fat man nodded to himself, then said, "It is always a pleasure to size up a godlike man who can only be described as obese. There is so much to size up. One could size him up for days and be continually amazed at all the nuances one would discover. I like you because so far I have sincerely enjoyed sizing you up. I will like you for a long time unless you interfere with my work, whatever my work happens to be at the moment." As if to answer the lawyer's unvoiced questions, he sat in one of the red leather chairs and crossed his legs below the knees, holding his Borsalino in his lap.

"I second the motion," said the demon, fondling his penis.

The lawyer sighed; clearly there was nothing he could do. Sitting in the remaining leather chair, he said, "I third it."

"I am gratified that at least two of you like me," said the

121

other fat man. "I am above mere like and dislike, but at least our relationship will not be an unpleasant one."

The witty leg man snorted. "Get it on; get it on!"

The other fat man snorted in return. "I will not be hounded. I realize that one of your duties is to hound me, but nevertheless I absolutely refuse to be hounded."

The witty leg man raised his eyebrows. "Sometimes you confuse even me."

"I know," said the other fat man, "and I find that most gratifying. I suppose I will 'get it on,' as you put it. There is nothing else to do and I want to be free to do nothing."

"Then why don't you tell us why you wanted to see us?" asked the lawyer, pressing the button on his sword-cane and rubbing the blade, being careful not to cut his fingers. He knew it would be another social blunder to stain the yellow rug red.

"Because your quite unexpected ambitions have surprised me, and I am upset by surprise. Because you represent the worst of the past, and I prefer the best of everything. Because our race is not mere man; the gift from the bems can never be taken away; and depression is mere man's ailment. And many other reasons, I assure you, but most of all because of what I am sure the witty leg man told you: I run the whole show. I run it; I want to see only what I like; and I do not want to have to look too often."

Strains of self-righteousness and malice ran through the other fat man's emotionless voice; at least that was what the lawyer believed. Those strains made him shiver despite himself. He wiped sweat from his brow and sent it to the anti-matter universe. He was sick of shivering despite himself, but he was also sick of covering up his faults. If his purpose was indeed to emulate mere man, then he had no reason to cover up his faults. So for once he simply shivered, content with his rather suspect rationalization. The truth was that the other fat man was an extremely confident godlike man; he was without a doubt the most powerful of all. The lawyer knew he would never win a showdown with him. The lawyer was surprised when he saw that the demon and the fat man were unimpressed with his statement.

Frowning in thought, the fat man conjured a glass of lemonade. He offered it to the lawyer, who refused. Smiling with satisfaction, he swallowed the lemonade in one noisy gulp. He lit his pipe and made the smoke smell like gasoline. He glanced at the other fat man, who pretended to ignore his lack of manners.

The witty leg man, who previously had been taking notes of the conversation in shorthand, stopped and held his right palm over his mouth, a gesture intended to make the others believe he, too, was deep in thought, but which in actuality was used to conceal his utter shock at the fat man's antics.

The demon, as usual, sat in the air, pulling at a nipple with one hand, fondling his penis with another.

The other fat man then did something the witty leg man had rarely seen him do: he lost control. No one was sure if he was acting or not, but that did not matter; the purpose, to intimidate his guests, was the same. Of course, he lost control in an eccentric fashion. He calmly pointed at the demon's penis and said, "Please refrain from ejaculating on my rug. It would be unclean."

"Please don't worry, friend other fat man," said the demon. "I never ejaculate."

The other fat man wanted to say, "Pfui," but he was afraid he could not articulate it clearly. He did not move except to fold his hands; he concentrated on maintaining his emotionless expression; he did not want them to learn of his confusion and inner turmoil.

Hadn't they realized he was trying to cow them?

He could not deduce answers, and he was not about to ask. He glanced at the witty leg man, hoping to find a clue from him. But the witty leg man was staring at the fat man smugly brushing imaginary dust from his white jacket. The other fat man leaned back in his chair. He then realized that previous guests had always been so impressed with his presence that they were cowed even as he opened his mouth, and yet these three were acting as they always did; that was the answer he was looking for, and it had shocking implications. These three possessed a confidence alien to all other godlike men; they were totally convinced of their ultimate victory; despite their godlike powers, they resembled mere man in that they would let nothing stop them, even if victory led them to their doom.

All this reasoning took five seconds, an unusual amount of time for the other fat man. His guests were not unaware of it. At least he knew what to do: he had to frighten them into submission, even if it meant revealing his innermost secrets.

"I must thank you for setting the matter straight," said the other fat man. "Not in my wildest dreams would I have thought that such a huge organ could be put to no practical purpose. Were I the sort to envy organs, I might have indeed envied it, but certainly not now.

"However, your attitude betrays the fact that you are unaware that I possess a certain quality which sets me apart from you, which amplifies my abilities, and which enables me to perceive things you could never perceive. That quality is—genius. Of all the godlike man, I am the only one who is more intelligent than anyone else. Naturally, when the opportunity to rule Earth presented itself, I took advantage of it. However, I prefer to spend most of my time with my black orchids. I am sure you understand; they are such lovely flowers."

"But how do we know you rule?" asked the lawyer. "The race of godlike man has fifty-seven kings, thirty-eight queens, and a pretender, not counting the Queen of England they all acknowledge as their superior. Why don't you tell us of the things you have done that the Virgin Queen can't do?"

The other fat man said, "The custom of selecting identities rather than searching for one's own is an innovation of mine. I simply implanted the thought in the people's minds before they could learn what they could do with their powers. My success was greater than I had anticipated. For instance, the lawyer is now the lawyer, and he has no memories of ever having had an identity other than that of the lawyer. The same is true of everyone."

The fat man rubbed his cheek. He shifted position in his chair; it was clear that he had spent too much time sitting down lately and his buttocks were falling asleep again. "Why, that is metaphysically absurd!"

"What it sounds like to you does not matter," replied the other fat man. "But nevertheless, it *is* the truth. Rarely have I found it necessary to influence a godlike man's life so he would not have doubts, and only once have I been forced to extreme measures to protect our culture."

"And what were those measures?" asked the lawyer.

The other fat man waved his hand as if to dismiss the

question. "It was nothing for a godlike man of my genius. All it required was sending the buildings around Carter Hall to the anti-matter universe." He paused for an instant and glanced at the witty leg man. "Are you getting all this down?"

"Have I ever failed you before?" asked the witty leg man, writing out his own question.

The other fat man snorted; his guests were not sure what the snort meant. Floating toward the other fat man's desk, the demon asked, "And just what is so great about our past that you do not want to see it die?"

The other fat man's lips twisted upward a bit; that was his version of a smile. "My fondest memories are of Earth before the various holocausts that destroyed most of mere man: be to exact, of Cleveland in 1950. I was but a child then, and spent most of my time in my parents' apartment. That is why so many of you live in apartments; I happen to like them." His attention faltered; his eyes darted about the room as if he was searching for an object shrouded in mist. "I wonder what those holocausts were. It was so long ago."

The demon, the lawyer, and the fat man looked at each other in confusion. Drumming his fingers on his stomach, the fat man squinted his eyes so he could see only the layers of fat rippling under his white suit; the light was finally bothering him. He lowered his head and his fat neck smothered his collar. "Friend other fat man," he said, "it has occurred to me that despite your imposing size, you are a narrow godlike man."

The witty leg man stared at his desk; it was difficult for him to hold onto his pen. The lawyer raised an eyebrow. The demon rubbed his chin with his tongue.

The other fat man's eyes ceased wandering, but they still seemed unable to focus on an object. "I am not narrow," he said. "It is true that the years are beginning to take their toll. It must be sad to see a genius become senile before your very eyes so—please—do not emote in my presence. You have my permission to emote after our little meeting is over and you are back in your apartments." He blinked and regained total control of himself. "I am the only godlike man in existence who fully realizes the meaning of immortality. That knowledge weighs heavily upon me. Although I have spent most of my life resting, I sometimes yearn for a more permanent rest. All of which means I sometimes suffer relapses. One of the witty leg man's jobs is to prevent them whenever possible. You should be thankful that I have imposed order upon your lives, otherwise you too would be cursed with unavoidable stupors."

The fat man breathed deeply. He lifted his head, puffed his pipe (the smoke smelled like rotten bananas), and pointed at the other fat man. "You claim you have imposed order; you claim to know much of the truth. Then tell me this: who am I?"

The lawyer rubbed his hands in glee. "Good! I just love riddles; they're so easy to solve!"

"Then solve this one," said the other fat man. "What difference does it make?"

The lawyer pursed his lips. "Is it greater than twenty-six?"

"Much less, friend lawyer," said the demon, floating closer to the witty leg man.

"Indeed," said the fat man, crossing and uncrossing his ankles in a futile attempt to pump more blood into his buttocks. "I think he is trying to tell us that the answer is zero."

"Zero?" asked the lawyer. "What kind of answer is that?"

"The wrong one," said the demon. "The other fat man is implying that we should be content to play our little games on our little planet, instead of facing great dangers in the stars, daring all, risking all, chasing one goal after another, never completely satisfied, yet always with hope! I, for one, don't like it!" Tapping the witty leg man on the shoulder, he said, "Are you getting all this down, or am I going too fast for you?"

The witty leg man clenched his hands into fists and shook them. "Why is everybody doubting my considerable abilities today?"

"Who cares?" asked the lawyer.

"A pointed question, but a good one nevertheless," said the fat man. "There are very few good questions which do not allow the recipient to hem and haw and hedge. It is a good question because today will see historic consequences. After today every godlike man will be looking after his own interests, without someone mysteriously guiding him along the 'proper path.' And fortunately we three are together. We will stand together forever! We will not fail!"

The other fat man sighed; only incredibly exasperating circumstances such as these could make him ignore the fact that it was time for supper. He said, "It is my firm belief that we should discuss the subjects at hand; all others are of no concern to me."

"Of course," said the fat man. "I understand. I only wish you could explain your position in full detail. I would like to know more of why you have schemed to make the race of godlike man unaware of its full power and potential. As near as you can remember it, anyway."

"And you can say you're sorry, too," said the lawyer.

Forming a steeple with his hands, the other fat man leaned forward. Unused to seeing him in actiom, the lawyer was afraid that he would lean too hard and too far, until he toppled over, his great bulk crashing into his cherrywood desk and breaking it into splinters and sawdust. No such thing happened. In fact, the other fat man leaned forward quite gracefully. He said:

"You should trust your ruler to know what is best for you, even if he is a secret ruler. I know I would, if I were less than what I am. And you should be grateful for your serene existence, because using your full power and potential is a heartbreaking affair. You would have fun for an eon or so, but then you would grow bored; you would have done everything you could have imagined possible. And I *should* know. After I had established order on this planet, I went around the universe, causing what trouble I could. I created some very unusual things, including the crawling bird, that pathetic little creature you encountered when you began your heretical enterprise to return depression to this planet. I even created several humanoid races, such as the one ruled by the Ebony Kings." He snorted. "What humorous lackeys they are!" He stared at the lawyer.

Holding tightly to his sword-cane, the lawyer tried to ignore the other fat man's stare. He knew that the other fat man had successfully deduced that he was the weak link in the trio. He cleared his throat. "Then may I take it that you're about to come to the point of this meeting?" he asked, unable to hide the quiver in his voice.

"I am not one for dilly-dallying when it is unnecessary," said the other fat man. "However, I am sure that you know what I am talking about."

The lawyer looked to the demon and the fat man for support; apparently unconcerned, they were looking at the ceiling. The lawyer realized that the ball had been tossed into his lap and that it would stay there. He stood his sword-cane on the floor and leaned on it, trying not to sway back and forth due to his nervousness. "Er, ah, ahem, I assume you want to make a deal."

"Do I look like the type who makes deals?"

"You never know," said the lawyer. "If you want us to become inactive, or to direct our energies elsewhere. . . ." He noticed that the demon and the fat man had stopped staring at the ceiling and were now staring at him. He was thankful that the witty leg man was still doing his job, otherwise *all* the eyes in the room would have been upon him. "Uh, then you have to make it worth our while." The lawyer was visibly relieved when he saw a faint smile come to the fat man's lips.

"I have your lives," said the other fat man.

"Huh?" asked the lawyer. "Where?"

The other fat man looked down at his palms; the meaning of that significant gesture was not lost on the lawyer.

"Oh. There," said the lawyer. He licked his lips. "Could you give me Kitty, too?"

"I can't believe I heard that," said the demon.

"You heard it," said the fat man.

"Do you two wish to add something?" asked the other fat man. His tone showed that he was becoming quite satisfied with himself.

"No. Quite the contrary," said the demon.

"You are doing well enough without our help," said the fat man.

"Well then, friend lawyer, is there anything else you want?" asked the other fat man. "I could allow you to suffer abject depression, if that is what you wish. It is within my power and will cost me only a small effort."

The witty leg man ceased taking notes and cleared his throat.

"I apologize. It will cost the witty leg man a small effort. He has many of my abilities, you see."

The lawyer smiled and relaxed. "No. I don't think I'm ready for another bout with abject depression yet. Kitty is another matter." He glanced at the demon. "Do you think we'll be happy together?"

The demon shrugged. "Certainly. If you like sleeping with the Big Red Cheese."

"That was an unkind remark," said the lawyer.

"I'm just stating the facts."

Once again the other fat man ignored the interruption; it was going to be a good day after all; he was already calling himself a silly old fool for doubting himself earlier. He knew that it was time to wrap up this affair quickly and chalk up another victory to his genius. "Of course you are speaking for your friends, too?"

"We three will stick together no matter what," said the lawyer.

"Then should you agree, tomorrow I will set in motion certain cosmic forces. By next week Kitty will be in your arms; she will be panting and lusting after your kisses." A sickened look passed over the fat man's face.

"I agree!"

"Then may we consider the deal closed?"

Before the lawyer could say yes, before the witty leg man could put down his pen, the fat man jumped in the air and landed with a resounding thud. The lawyer assumed that his buttocks had fallen fast asleep and that he had chosen this inopportune moment to alleviate his condition. He changed his mind when the fat man exclaimed:

"You are a good dog, lawyer! I could not have done a better job myself!"

The demon applauded. "If there was room for me to stand, friend lawyer, I would give you a standing ovation!"

The fat man lumbered to the demon and held out his right hand palm upward. The demon leaned down and slapped the fat man's hand. Then the fat man slapped the demon's hand.

"We did it!" exclaimed the demon.

"It was no contest!" said the fat man.

The witty leg man bit the tip of his pen, ignoring the bitter taste of the ink. The other fat man watched the proceedings closely; he sensed his world shattering.

His eyes to the floor, the lawyer reviewed the latest developments; he could find no logic in them. He blinked several times, thinking that if he blinked enough he would wake up in his apartment, theoretically refreshed after a long sleep but, in reality, uneasy due to some strange dream. He gestured to the fat man, who lumbered to him and bent over so he could whisper in his ear, "What did we do?"

The fat man slapped the lawyer on the shoulder, almost sending him flying from his chair. "The demon and I should have been more precise. It is not what we did, but what you did that counts!"

"Me?"

"Who else could have done it?" asked the fat man.

"I could have on my better days," said the demon, "but I might have become overconfident; my chuckles would have given me away."

"What did I do?"

"That is my question," said the other fat man, signalling the witty leg man to resume taking notes.

"Why, it is so obvious that I am disappointed that you have to ask," said the fat man, sitting down and crossing his ankles in one smooth, exaggerated motion.

"At this point in time, I do not care what you think of me," said the other fat man.

"Never?" asked the demon.

"Not to my recollection. I simply want some answers."

"He lulled you into a sense of security," said the fat man. "He played a magnificent game. Until the last possible instant it looked as if he would capitulate to your outrageous demands. You were an immense cat, ready to pounce upon your victory. And he yanked it away from you! What a sight it was to behold!" The fat man paused for a moment to chuckle, as if the entire conference had been a private joke. "Friend lawyer, your shenanigans never cease to amaze me!"

"He is deep, isn't he?" asked the demon.

"He most certainly is," answered the fat man. "Every time I see him, I contemplate his deepness. He is like the ocean itself, ever-changing, yet somehow always the same."

"Uh, there're a few points I'd like to clear up," said the lawyer.

"Of course," said the demon.

"I'd like to know why the fact that he—" the lawyer gestured toward the other fat man, "—holds our lives in the palms of his hands is so unimportant. I was under the impression that he could make us shuffle off whenever it pleased him."

"Oh. That!" said the demon.

"It is easily explained," said the fat man.

"Yes," said the other fat man. "I too am most interested in the reasoning behind your peculiar reaction to my life-and-death hold over you."

"We don't believe you have a hold," said the demon.

"You are insane, you poor deluded godlike man," said the fat man. "Perhaps the shrink can help you. He does not have regular office hours and he does not like to keep appointments, but I am sure he can make an exception in your case."

"Your remarks are hardly comforting," said the other fat man, "especially when you consider the fact that I do not believe I am deluded."

"It's always like that when people go nuts," said the demon, making no attempt to conceal the pity in his voice.

"They think they are sane and everyone else is insane," said the fat man.

"Yes, I can see it all now," said the demon. "When mere man became godlike man, it was too much for your wretched mind to bear. Life had changed too suddenly for you. When you discovered that you could not retrace your steps, you basked in the glory of your power, overcompensating for your sense of loss." He shook his head. "Even that didn't soothe your pain. From there I can only speculate. Because everybody else appeared to be playing meaningless games, you decided that you would too. You woke one morning fancying that the chaos you saw about you was of your own creation; you believed yourself to be the ruler of Earth. All that remained was to convince the godlike men who would become your witty leg man and your cook. And here you are now, residing in this quaint structure and reinforcing your madness. *Folie á deux*. You're in extremely poor condition."

The fat man nodded in approval. "Friend demon," he said solemnly, "not even the shrink could have done better."

"I know," said the demon.

For an instant the other fat man's face expressed confusion and panic, but then his features softened and his thin lips twisted upward. "If you do not believe me, how else do you explain the sudden rise of godlike mankind and the weirdness of our culture?"

"I didn't presume to explain it," said the demon, "and I really don't care how it started. I just wanted to explain your madness."

"What if I decided to prove the existence of my life-and-death hold over you three by destroying the lawyer?"

The lawyer stood up and shook his fist at the other fat man. "Why, that's the most outrageous thing I've ever heard! You wouldn't dare!"

"How do you know?" asked the other fat man.

"I can answer your question with a question," said the fat man, motioning the lawyer to sit down, "and that question is: what difference does it make?"

By this time the witty leg man had stopped taking notes. He had been holding his pen tightly. When the fat man voiced his question, the witty leg man accidently snapped the pen. He was in such a state of shock that he was not startled by the sudden noise, and he continued sitting motionless, waiting for his employer's response to the fat man's question.

The other fat man merely leaned over and scowled. "What do you mean?"

"A godlike man is not a ruler if his subjects do not obey him," said the fat man. "And he is not a secret ruler if his subjects do not believe him when they are confronted with the information. You have no power over us simply because we have elected not to believe you. Is that not correct, friend lawyer?"

"Uh, that's right," said the lawyer, running his words together. "I was toying with you, friend other fat man." He pressed the button of his sword-cane and pointed it at the other fat man in an attempt to look as menacing as possible. When he noticed that his pose was having no effect, he slowly lowered his sword-cane. He wished that he was safe at home.

"But the lawyer's death would be a fact that you could not ignore," said the other fat man confidently.

"Perhaps. Perhaps not," said the fat man. "If you destroyed him, my gunsel would impersonate him forever if it would make me happy. I could ignore his death quite easily under those circumstances. But again, the truth is that it makes no difference. You will not kill the lawyer to prove a point; you are not a godlike man of action."

"You have me there. I do not want to kill the lawyer."

"And it's a good thing, too," said the lawyer.

The demon pricked his finger on his beak and accidently scratched his delicate green skin with his long red fingernail. "Even if you are the secret ruler of Earth, even if your grasp on reality isn't tenuous—and that's a far-fetched assumption—we've planted the seeds of doubt in your mind. Now you're just like all the other godlike men. There'll be times when you'll stop tending your black orchids; you'll look up into the starry sky; and you'll say, 'What is reality?' "

"What is reality?" asked the lawyer, his curiosity aroused.

The fat man stood up and bowed. "And upon that paradoxical note, friend other fat man, we will take our leave."

On the way out the lawyer thumbed his nose at the witty leg man; the witty leg man placed his right hand in the crook of his left elbow. The other fat man would have said, "Pfui," but he did not feel like making the slightest move. He did not even feel like rushing to the dining room when he heard the cook locking the front door after the demon had floated out behind his friends. The witty leg man opened his mouth to speak to him, and it was only through concentrated effort that the other fat man said, "Do not talk to me until tomorrow. Otherwise I am certain that I will suffer a relapse."

5. The other fat man did not quite suffer a relapse; he exercised self-control; he did not want to divorce himself from the questions nagging at him. True, he did brood; instead of sleeping, he spent the night tending his black orchids. Although his supper of oysters baked in the shell, terrapin Maryland, beaten biscuits, pan-broiled young turkey, rice croquettes with quince jelly, lima beans in cream, sally lunn, avocado todhunter, pineapple sherbert, sponge

133

cake, Wisconsin dairy cheese, and Sumatran blue mountain coffee had been delicious—as was to be expected—he had found it difficult to eat at all. And as he brooded, alone in his greenhouse, he suffered an upset stomach, one of the early signs that a relapse was imminent.

He did not brood on the question of his madness; if he believed that the demon and the fat man were correct, it would not help him solve his immediate predicament. For whatever the reasons, his real or imagined reign was drawing to a close.

The other fat man knew that he could have proven that he was not mad if he had destroyed the lawyer; it would have been a simple, yet devastating gesture. There would have been no proper way for him to rationalize his position as a protector of godlike mankind if he had wantonly slain a helpless entity merely to consolidate that position. He may have been misguided, but he most certainly was not evil; not even the godlike men in the lowest social strata were evil; he had seen to that (or so he believed) long ago. Besides, one of his favorite sayings was, "A godlike man may exile nonsense from the library of his reason, but not from the arena of his impulses." To have slain the lawyer would have been a nonsensical act of reason, and the witty leg man never would have stopped kidding him about it.

All this brooding was extremely confusing to the other fat man; he was thinking along lines alien to him. Often he felt that he was reaching an ultimate conclusion, its brilliance smacking of his unique genius; but then he would feel as though he were walking a path leading to many other paths. And somehow, no matter which path he took, he would always conclude his walk in the same place he had begun. It was a most distressing sensation; he was not used to prolonged convoluted reasoning; his genius had heretofore allowed him to avoid it.

He realized that due to his unnerving, complex thoughts, his gardening was reflexive; near dawn he realized that he would have to stop if he was not to damage any of his black orchids. In days past, if the witty leg man had suggested that it was remotely within the realm of possibility, he would have pfui'ed him out of the room; and here he was, about to do so. The orchids were frail; if he held a pedal too tightly, then the color would fade or run; he might puncture a vein and the perfection of its structure would be lost forever. And the orchids were delicate; the flower might wither and die, and not even all of his considerable power could save it. The other fat man mulled over that thought for a time, even though he suspected it of being maudlin; but he had always paid more attention to little things than to large ones.

Truly this was a night for him to remember; he had forgotten what it was like to feel hopeless and sad, to be depressed. Not since Cleveland in 1950 had he been so depressed. And yet those were the years he loved so much. Was it possible to become sentimental over depression?

The other fat man scowled at this question, even as he chuckled over it. He looked toward the roof of the greenhouse; he inexplicably searched for a glimpse of the stars. Because of the sunlamps shining on his black orchids he could not see them. He was disappointed.

New thoughts came to him; it had been so long since he had seen the stars. He wanted to know why he had wanted to look. When he had been a mere man, looking at them had always made him feel small; his most grandiose visions of his self-importance paled before them. Yet the stars had also made him feel as if he were a significant part of the universe. Despite their chill, they had provided warmth.

He willed the sunlamps off, and he was drenched in a comforting darkness. His futile attempts to maintain his power seemed a dream now. He thought of the cook and the witty leg man; they were asleep; he realized that when he made his plans, he would have to provide for them. The knowledge of that responsibility was comforting, but mostly there was the darkness. There was a peace in the darkness he could never understand while contemplating in the light, and he wished that he could experience it alone, surrounded by his black orchids, sheltered by his ivory tower; forever.

But the darkness would not last forever. With the dawn came a desire to make a decision, any decision that would lead to activity. Perhaps an activity of madness would do. Perhaps taking a path contrary to everything he had ever believed he stood for was the proper medicine, the proper solution for the many things puzzling him. Perhaps if he once again traveled among the stars. Perhaps if he once again created something from nothingness, if he gave shape and substance to a thought.

He decided that he would not go alone this time. He would request—definitely not order—the witty leg man and the cook to accompany him. He knew they would, but he wanted them to *want* to go.

The other fat man realized, as he walked toward the elevator, that the demon, the lawyer, and the fat man were not totally wrong after all. For some godlike men, depression was benign; hopelessness brought hope. But the other fat man was not a common godlike man, and he knew that the trio would have many lessons to learn about common godlike men.

He did not think of that for very long. Since today was a special occasion he decided that he would fix a breakfast of orange juice, eggs *au beurre noir,* six slices of broiled Georgia ham, hashed brown potatoes, hot blueberry muffins, and a pot of steaming cocoa. While he served the cook and the witty leg man breakfast for the first time, he would discuss his plans with them.

Already he looked forward to exploring the universe with them.

6. The fat man, having concluded his deep knee-bends, slapped his rump just hard enough to make his hand tingle. "Ah, it feels better now." Wiping the sweat from his forehead and neck with a white towel, he sat down in the Morris chair. He slid back and forth until he was comfortable. When the demon returned from taking out the garbage, the fat man said, "Ah. I repeat, ah. My brain is signaling my nerves to register pleasure. It is sad, friend demon, that you do not sit as I do; you can never know the joy of sitting without concentration."

The lawyer turned away and looked out the picture window. He stood with his hands behind his back and his legs apart. He vividly recalled the days when he could sit in the Morris chair whenever he wanted to. He decided to be nasty. It was a moment of wild abandon; he thought he might be risking his relationship with his two friends if he drew attention to himself so soon after he had almost given up his quest for depression. "It looks as if you're going to sit there for a long time," he said, his back still to the fat man.

"I don't understand," said the demon, licking his hands clean.

"Whether or not we actually uncovered the truth from the other fat man is immaterial," the lawyer said, "but the point remains that we've no other place to look. I, for one, have no ideas."

"Many times I've agreed with that remark," said the demon, dusting a tiny sculpture of the demon Belial presenting his credentials to Solomon. He sniffed the feather duster.

"That was a nasty thing to say," said the lawyer, his face reddened with anger. He turned around and paced the room; he swung his sword-cane, hoping to accidently smash something. He accidently smashed his knee. As he hopped about in pain, he uttered pathetic little groans.

The demon said, "You should have been more careful. And you should have listened more carefully to the other fat man instead of dreaming of Kitty."

The fat man chuckled. The lawyer said, "Now that's an unfair remark! Didn't the two of you tell him that I was just leading him on? You admitted it yourself! Or are you going to tell me that he was telling the truth about everything?"

"Whether or not I believe he was telling the truth about everything is immaterial," said the demon with a glint in his eye. "And I, for one, will never tell you the truth, because I'd rather you wondered about it. However, the point remains that the other fat man may have told us the truth about *some* things; he may have told us where to look."

The lawyer forgot that he was angry; he smiled. "Where?"

"Do you not recall what the other fat man said about the bems thrusting the gift of godhood upon mere man?" asked the fat man.

The lawyer nodded. Thinking back to the conference, he could recall only his fright and his desire for Kitty; he wanted his friends to think he remembered the other fat man's statement, so he did not ask for more details. He walked back to the picture window. He was bathed in blue.

A thought occurred to him. "Listen to me. If the bems are powerful enough to turn mere men into gods, then aren't they also powerful enough to take away those powers, if the whim strikes them?"

The demon shrugged; he was full of satanic confidence.

"Do not worry," said the fat man. "You knew the job was dangerous when you took it."

SLICES OF LIFE: FOUR

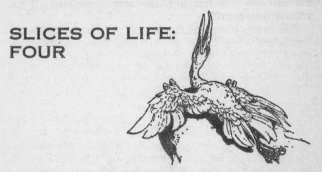

The mature eternal child watched the sunset as he sat under an elm tree; his hands were cupped behind his head and, although he had convinced himself that he was very comfortable, his hands hurt; the bark had scraped the skin around his knuckles. He appeared relaxed. If he could have kept his mind on the sunset's red and gold rays, the cool air, and the soft green grass of the park, he might, in reality, have been relaxed. He might have forgotten his past and his future; there would have been only the present and he would have been purged of the internal conflicts obsessing him. He would have enjoyed the battle between the two flying squirrels, fighting for a mate who apathetically searched for nuts and berries; and the Big Red Cheese escorting a godlike woman and loudly proclaiming his ridiculous philosophies that had infatuated so many and which no one who called himself educated could ignore; and the arias of the birds; and the pleasant odor of lemon-scented flowers; and the laughing eternal children running about their playground, making him yearn for the days which he believed he had enjoyed immensely, but which, in reality, he had spent in fear and misery, cursing the lonely hawkman.

He wished that he had the ability to create a nice cold drink or a hot roast beef sandwich; he imagined that eating a good meal in the plesant surroundings of the park would be conducive to the digestive process. He knew that if he ate, he would have an upset stomach unless he did something to soothe the guilt feelings nagging him, preventing him from enjoying the luxuries he considered to be his birthright. He was sorry that he had cursed the hawkman; he had spent most of the day searching for him before he had reluctantly come to the conclusion that whatever had happened to Carter Hall had happened to the hawkman, too. The mature eternal child did not know if the hawkman had ever been aware of his cursing, but nevertheless he felt that he should make amends for abusing the godlike man.

He also felt guilty because he had left home. After all the solemn promises to himself that he would force his parents to accept him as a mature eternal child, he had given up in less than a week. He did not care to think of the scene of his leaving; it had been a nasty fight. When his parents finally acknowledged his altered appearance, they threatened to turn him back into the child they had known and loved. He did not know if they could undo what the shrink's machines had accomplished, but he did not want to take the chance; his maturity was too precious. He insulted his parents, called them fouler names than he had called the hawkman; he dared them to do their worst; and he laughed aloud as he walked through the door. He laughed and laughed as he walked down the hall to the elevator.

Inside the elevator his mood had sobered; he thought that he should cry, but he had no desire to do so. He thought that he should feel guilty; after all, they had sheltered him for eons. And paradoxically, he felt guilty because he did not feel guilty; some part of him would not admit that his break with them was for the best.

The mature eternal child wondered what he should do about his future. The sun had disappeared behind mountains now traced with a yellow glow; in a few moments there would be no glow and the darkness would rapidly smother the world. The mature eternal child smiled; soon he would look at the moon and the stars. The birds would stop singing their arias; the flying squirrels would stop chattering; the eternal children would go home for supper; the Big Red Cheese would end his monologue as he became engrossed in personal matters. The entire park would be silent.

The mature eternal child decided that what he did about his future did not matter, as long as he did *something*. If he spent the next decade in the park, if he lived in silence by night and in joyous noise by day, if he were content, then nothing else mattered. He could be a tramp, a counselor at the nearby camp for eternal children, a practical joker, a philosopher; for the first time he realized he could be anything; for the first time the thought of his future did not fill him with anxiety but, instead, set him free.

The mature eternal child closed his eyes and breathed deeply, waiting for the night to come.

CHAPTER FIVE

1. The lawyer had not known that the job would be dangerous when he had taken it; he went into space with the demon and the fat man not because he had willfully gone into danger with them many times before, but because he was afraid they would accept his fear without trying to talk him into being brave and, consequently, would leave him behind.

The fat man wanted to see the sights of outer space, so they did not teleport directly from world to world; standing as if they were casually leaning on a lamppost, waiting for a streetcar, they traveled at eight million light-years per second. The fat man smiled slightly; the demon's head was turned around one hundred and eighty degrees so no one could see his expression.

Smoking a cigarette, the lawyer wondered how they could remain calm with the spectacle of space surrounding them, the gleaming, tiny stars surrounding them. They flew between the galaxies; blurs silently whipped past them. When his cigarette was smoked to the filter, the lawyer sent the butt to the anti-matter universe. Perhaps his friends were not calm, he thought; perhaps they were meditating on the joys of the universe; perhaps they were experiencing a delightful fear in their gut that made them savor every charming, dangerous moment. Perhaps, unlike the lawyer, they did not indicate it. But what reason did they have for hiding their feelings?

The lawyer did not ponder the question long. He realized

that he felt like an eternal child riding a ferris wheel whirling through complex configurations of time; the hint of danger never materialized; he could risk his life and beat the odds without effort; every fiber of his godlike being was excited at the pleasant motion, the temporary alteration of reality which expanded his mental horizons without causing him to think deeply. The lawyer had not had so much fun since the last time Kitty had paid attention to him. Finally, he could no longer hoard the jewels of dialogue occurring to him; he just had to share his exultation with his friends. Unfortunately he had been serious ever since the beginning of the quest; it was no longer his habit to be carefree; so he asked:

"In what direction are we traveling? Straight up?"

The demon turned his head around; he sighed. "Friend lawyer, why did you have to distract me? I was having a good time wondering what Cleveland must have been like in 1950."

The fat man rested his hands on his stomach and said, "Likewise, I am sure. And to answer your question, there is no direction in outer space."

"Then where are we going? You two never confide in me any more."

"That's your imagination," said the demon. "But to answer your revised question, we're nearing the planet of the Ebony Kings. Perhaps they know something of the bems."

"And where's the gunsel?" asked the lawyer. "I don't see him."

The fat man chuckled; not at the lawyer, but at the coldness of space. "He is around."

"Oh." The lawyer smiled. "Isn't it wonderful?" he asked, gesturing at the distant stars. "I've never done this before! I didn't know it could be so wonderful!"

"It *is* wonderful," declared the fat man solemnly.

"I like it," said the demon.

"That's what I really wanted to talk to you about!" said the lawyer, grinning so widely that he was almost embarassed.

"Then why didn't you say so?" asked the demon.

"I was having so much fun that I was encountering difficulty keeping my thoughts in order," said the lawyer. "I was accidently serious."

"Quite understandable," said the fat man, raising his eyebrows.

"It's been a long time since the demon and I have had fun together. And I've never had fun with you, friend fat man. Traveling among the stars with you is an experience! Don't ask me why."

Chuckling louder than before, the fat man smiled at the demon, then at the lawyer, who was amazed at how friendly an unctuous smile could be. The lawyer smiled at his friends; then he chuckled. The demon did not merely chuckle; he laughed, all five meters of his body shaking with his mirth. The lawyer and the fat man also laughed.

They laughed for a long time, at first because of the sheer release of it; then because they were thinking about what a sight they were—a demon, a lawyer, and a fat man, standing straight up and traveling eight million light-years per second; and finally, simply because they were laughing.

2. The demon, the lawyer, and the fat man visited the planet of the Ebony Kings for a half hour, though the demon wished the stay could have been extended. The planet had a red sky that reminded him of caked blood; black clouds spotted the sky. A native remarked to the demon that he had never seen a day when the sky was clear. The castles of the Ebony Kings were in the center of a valley; all the distant mountains were live volcanoes which constantly spat ashes into the air. Although the lawyer and the fat man created gas masks for themselves, the demon breathed the air without any sort of filter; he thought its refreshing odor well-suited to his tastes.

The demon especially liked the talking, blood-sucking gray flowers growing between the cracks in the sidewalks outside the Ebony Kings' castles. Another native told him that the kings had spent all the taxes they had collected for twenty years to eliminate the flowers so they could take early morning walks and ponder the affairs of state without interruption; the Kings had, however, succeeded only in defoliating their victory gardens. Confused, the demon wondered if there was another rationale for destroying such lovely creatures; if not, then he was certain that the Ebony Kings were witless, unperceptive fools.

He spent twenty minutes discussing satanic pleasures with a flower of particulary impressive intelligence. The demon told the flower all about the time he had possessed the saintly godlike man with holes in his hands and feet and had made him recite obscenities and succumb to repressed sexual desires (such as pinching the Queen of England's rump); all about the time he had made the sun rise in the west; all about the time he had convinced the dirty old man that the young female eternal children were only after his body, that they did not care for his mind or his godlike powers; and all about the time he had masqueraded as the doctor and operated on the quarterback's knees, telling him later that he would never to be able to pass again. And the flower told the demon all about the time he had bitten the ankle of an Ebony King, making him jump nine meters in the air and causing him to lose a considerable amount of his dignity; all about the time he had defeated a scepter with a living, intelligent death's head on a quiz show which dealt with the subtleties of Spinoza; all about the time he had had too much blood to drink during a demonstration and had passed out; and all about the time an Ebony King had ruptured himself by trying to pull him from the sidewalk.

The demon was displeased when the conversation was cut short by the approach of the lawyer and the fat man. The lawyer bounced with each step. Sighing, the demon asked them what had happened during their visit to an Ebony King.

The fat man said, "It did not take much for me to convince him to talk; only a minor display of my awesome power."

"It seems there hasn't been a bem here for eons," said the lawyer. "The last one that visited this planet laughed at it because he thought it was tacky. Before he left he said he was going to Snarf because they had excellent mung there, and he was hungry."

The flower said, "Did you know that mung is the substance derived from beating a pregnant armadillo suffering from an acute case of space senility with a spiked baseball bat in 3/4 time? The mung is the substance that flows from the nose."

"Please. Not now," said the demon, whose green skin was tinged with yellow. He reluctantly added, "I suppose we'll have to leave now."

"Yes," said the lawyer. "And why not? This planet *is* tacky."

"Wait!" said the flower to the demon. "Before you leave, you must do one thing."

"And what's that?" asked the demon.

"Feed me," said the flower. "Feed me! Feed me! Feed me! Feedmefeedmefeedmefeedme!"

"I think that can be arranged, old friend," said the demon, creating a cut-glass punchbowl of blood on the sidewalk. "Drink it in good health."

The demon, the lawyer, and the fat man left at eight million light-years per second, utilizing a rhomboidal trajectory, not slackening their speed until they reached Snarf.

3. Snarf was a world characterized by air-breathing intelligent fish with tiny, thin arms and tinier, thinner legs. The fish loved to walk, although their legs were extremely weak and wobbled with their every step; the fish appeared to be in perpetual danger of toppling over, their legs under constant threat of snapping under the strain of supporting their weight; neither event ever happened.

The fish of Snarf loved to go on fifty kilometer hikes. Harnessed into their back-packs, they crawled out of the sea early in the morning and walked up the steepest mountains they could find until they collapsed in blissful exhaustion.

More than they loved to hike, however, the fish loved to dance. They danced on the seashore at night; they built huge bonfires by rubbing flint rocks together; and then they danced and danced and danced, holding hands, singing senseless songs, smiling their ugly fish-like smiles, and inventing clever new steps. When a fish invented a clever new step that was clearly beyond the ordinary, he knew it instantly because a feeling of warmth swept through him; he was no longer afraid of dancing so close to the fire that his body would become too dry for him to survive; he completely forgot the details of the black night and the flickering light on the seashore; he was only dimly aware of the fish around him, the female fish whose attention he desired, the friends whom he believed he was not good enough for, his base ambitions to rise in the social order, the hideous moments of despair during which he believed that he had no purpose in life, that after he died he would be forgotten. The instinctive joy in repeating his step for all his comrades to see was, for the moment, enough justification for his existence; he might invent a second clever new step beyond the ordinary another night, but the glory would always be unique; it would always be his most comforting memory: the creation of that step made him the center of the universe. All boundaries were dissolved, he could reach to whomever or whatever he wanted; indeed, that moment of creation was the most exciting, most fulfilling of all, surpassing even the pleasure he experienced in the most private moments he spent with his lovers.

And the other fish knew it too; many of them had experienced such moments; the rest yearned for the moments and envied those fish who had been lucky enough to transcend the captivity of their own bodies and become something more than mere fish. When they saw the new step they were happy for the creator, and they demanded that he repeat it again and again until they could imitate what became known as *his* step, until it became an important new addition to the list of their abilities, until they knew it so well that they could not imagine dancing without it in their repertoires. And they danced it all night long, until fish forgot to throw wood on the fire and it slowly died, until the black sky turned dark blue. They danced the new step until, one by one, they collapsed into the sand; they looked at the brightening sky and felt the world spin under them; they felt the sea lapping over them, calling them home; but they did not want to return because they did not want to leave the site of creation. They drew strength from creation, too. They took part of the creator's strength and made it their own; they, too, had new warm memories which would soothe them in times of dark despair.

4. The demon, the lawyer, and the fat man landed on Snarf at the conclusion of such a scene; the last dancing fish, who had invented a step which his comrades had proclaimed to be the cleverest new step of all, was about to collapse. As the fish staggered to an uncrowded section of the beach, he squinted his eyes at the rising sun; he expected to see its rays reaching toward him, providing his shivering body with warmth; but the sun was hidden by the silhouettes of three creatures, the likes of which he had never seen before. His blissful exhaustion shattered by fear, he fell to his knees; he wondered if, by inventing his new step, he had reached too far beyond the essence of fishness; perhaps his comrades had been more correct than they had known; perhaps he had unwittingly displayed hubris. There were legends of such events, legends of fish who had danced so well that the gods had spirited them to lands in which they were worthy to dwell.

"Don't take me," the fish said in a rasping voice; he needed a drink of salt water. "I want to stay on Snarf. I want to remain with my glory."

"Do not worry," said the fat man. "Believe me when I tell you that we do not want you with us; you are too strange for my taste. We only want some information."

"Then I'll tell you whatever you want to know. You see, just before she collapsed, a fish looked at me with soulful eyes; I could tell that she admired the perfection of my body. And if you took me away, then we wouldn't be able to get together and . . . and. . . ."

"Spare me the details," said the lawyer; talk of getting together always reminded him of Kitty. "Tell us if a bem has been here lately looking for mung to eat."

The fish looked sick. "Do you know what mung *is?*"

"Please, not now." It was the lawyer's turn to look sick. "I know what mung is."

"There hasn't been mung here for many years. We manufactured it only as a social service. And as you must know, manufacturing mung causes armadillos to undergo an incredible strain. Well, the last armadillo died before I was born."

"That's a load off my mind," said the lawyer, twirling his sword-cane and watching it glint in the sun. "But what about the bems?"

"Legend speaks of a bem visiting a world called Sharkosh," said the fish. "That's all I know."

"I've heard of it," said the demon. "That's where we go next."

And the trio disappeared, leaving the awed fish on his knees. The sun blinded the fish; it was familiar, so he continued to look at it until sleep overcame him.

5. Sharkosh was a world of fire. The fire was at once all colors and individual colors—red, green, yellow, white, black, purple, and all others. Sharkosh had no dense core, no oxygen, no combustible materials; it was simply fire, a tiny ball of fire orbiting a dead sun.

Although the world was extremely interesting to visitors, its inhabitants, furry little green balls who breathed, ate, and excreted fire, were bored. They reveled in their boredom.

When they took boring strolls and met an equally bored friend, instead of asking him if anything exciting had happened to him recently, they asked if life was sufficiently boring for him. If their bored friend said in a bored monotone that something had happened—if his wife had left him or died, if he had accidently been witty at a party, if he was in good spirits—then they felt regret (but not profound regret, for that would have broken the pattern of their humdrum existence). They measured out their lives in swallows of yellow and blue fire, and they would have been proud of their boring accomplishments had not their dry philosophers proclaimed the nursing of the ego to be sinful.

The furry balls of Sharkosh had legends, but their legends were not repeated from father to son to fascinate and entertain, or to explain the unfathomable riddles of the universe; they were repeated word-for-word, without the slightest variation, so people would not accidently say something original.

Usually the legends told of furry balls, mavericks, who went out of their way to cause events; the mavericks discovered that an exciting life upset their digestive systems and distracted their mental processes; the mavericks soon learned that the most intelligent furry ball was unprepared to cope with seemingly unrelated, illogical events, even if they had been, in part, caused by his doing. The mavericks always returned to their boring wives and boring children; their conversations consisted of dull topics—the plainness of yellow fire and how comforting it was to watch, the lecture that had put the audience to sleep, and how horrible life must be on other worlds where the inhabitants were not so bored and orderly.

The furry balls married as soon as they could find a mate of sufficiently monumental boringness; they did not search for a mate with exquisite hair or ugly hair, but for one with plain, boring hair; intelligent furry balls found it difficult to obtain a mate, but when they concealed their intelligence it was not difficult at all.

Jokes made the furry balls sick, just as perceptive political insights made them sick. The furry balls always elected the most boring candidate to office, though they planned things in each district so that no candidate, regardless of how perfectly dull he was, would win by a wide margin.

The dullest furry balls were those who gained the most social status, but again their lives were organized so that a furry ball was never dull enough to be considered extraordinarily dull.

6. The demon, the lawyer, and the fat man were not average tourists; when they came upon a new environment they were abel to assess it instantly and to determine if it held interest for them. This was especially true when they arrived inside the fires of Sharkosh. The lawyer spoke first:

"What in the name of sin? This place is *boring*!"

The demon nodded in agreement. "Dull," he said, "excruciatingly dull." The lawyer received no answer from the fat man because the fat man was snoring.

"We should get this over with," said the demon, shaking the fat man awake.

A furry ball swam past them. The lawyer wiped sweat from his brow and licked his hand. "I'm dehydrating!" He created an ice cube and swallowed it. "That's better."

"But not by much," said the demon, floating toward the furry ball. "When I said we should get this over with, I meant that we should get this over with."

"Does that mean what I think it means?" the lawyer asked the fat man.

"It means what you think it means," said the fat man. "And I should think that you would want to get this over with too, for I am most positive that these flames must represent the emotion you want Kitty to feel in her heart for you." Before the stunned lawyer could reply, the fat man smiled and added, "And that means what you think it means."

"Thank you," said the lawyer dryly. "For a moment there I was afraid you wouldn't clear up that rather confusing remark."

They turned their attention to the demon, who was holding up his finger in a vain attempt to gain the furry ball's notice, and was saying, "But I only want to speak with you. One question. Well, maybe two, and I'll be on my way."

The furry ball swam until he was hidden by the flames. "Snobbish, isn't he?" said the demon, placing his hands on his hips.

"What did he do that for?" asked the lawyer. "Didn't he see you?"

"Indeed, he did," said the demon. "He ignored me so nothing would happen to him today."

"Are all those furry balls going to be like that?" asked the lawyer. "Disgusting!"

The trio politely attempted to interrupt the dull musings of many furry balls; as they expected, they were completely ignored; they might have been lackluster yellow flames as far as the furry balls were concerned. The lawyer was the first to become impatient. He selected a furry ball, swam through the fires next to him, and screamed as loud as he could; with all his godlike power supporting his efforts, the lawyer's screams created a deafening din that caused the demon's huge ears to ring. The lawyer's ploy availed him

152

nothing: shaking in shock, the furry ball continued on his way.

The lawyer was upset, but since he did not know how else to react, he simply stared at the furry ball until it was hidden by the flames.

The fat man rubbed his chin. "This will require effort, but I see no other way."

" 'This'?" asked the lawyer. "What is 'this'?"

"My clever plan," said the fat man. "Friend lawyer, we must do something which these creatures could never expect in their dullest dreams. In fact, I must challenge you to a game of basketball." He turned and pointed at the demon. "You will be the referee."

The lawyer was about to question the worth of the fat man's peculiar plan when the demon silenced him with a gesture. For an instant the lawyer was tired of spending a good deal of his immortal life opening his mouth and saying nothing; he was about to say so when he decided that he would be better off helping the fat man to realize his plan. "What am I supposed to do?"

"Practice dribbling," said the fat man. He snapped his fingers.

7. Fire became solid. The furry balls of Sharkosh suddenly found themselves sitting on bleachers of solid fire; this was an astounding event which they could not ignore; consequently they did not try to resume their normal lives at once. The bleachers surrounded a shiny basketball court; the fat man stood in the middle of it; his arms raised as high as he could reach them without ripping his white suit, he said, "I am happy that all of you could take time out of your busy schedules to make it here today. Needless to say, the proceeds of this game will go to charity. You see, the planet Earth is in need of information, given freely. I am sure you understand."

"Let the game begin!" said the demon.

"You tell him, ref!" said the lawyer, hopping up and down to limber up. He made his black suit and derby disappear; he replaced them with a green t-shirt, red shorts, and Paisley sneakers. He leaped up and grabbed the basketball

153

which had just appeared in the demon's hand. He dribbled down the court till he reached the basket; he made a lay-up. Retrieving the ball, he passed it smoothly to the fat man. "I made that look easy, didn't I?" he asked.

"You made it look as if you left your wheelchair yesterday," replied the fat man. "Prepare yourself for defeat. I am in better condition than you. Remember, I do deep knee-bends."

From a place no one could pinpoint, someone cheered. The fat man smiled at the lawyer. "Ah, listen to the gunsel. It is gratifying to have faithful fans."

"Even faithful fans are fickle," said the lawyer. "We'll see whom he likes when the game's over!"

"Let the game begin!" said the demon, taking the basketball from the fat man, biting down on his whistle (being careful not to press too hard with the sharp edges of his beak), and floating to the circle, center court.

The fat man made his white suit and Borsalino disappear; he replaced them with a bright blue short sleeve shirt decorated with yellow flowers, and with Bermuda shorts to match. His sneakers were also blue. The fat man and the lawyer, ready to jump for the ball at any second, crouched inside the circle. The demon tossed the ball into the air and floated out of their way. The fat man and the lawyer jumped.

The great basketball game had begun.

And what a game it was! The lawyer proved himself to be the most magnificent dribbler in the history of the game. When he was in possession of the ball, his hands were a blur. He dribbled the ball between his legs, behind his back, seven centimeters from the court, with either hand; often he exchanged hands. The moves he put on the fat man were nothing short of fantastic. Even the fat man had to admit that the lawyer was a wizard of the court. The fat man marveled every time the lawyer pivoted and changed direction to keep his shots from being blocked. The lawyer could not be guarded. Sometimes it was as if he were the only person on the court, a godlike man who lived only for the pleasure of basketball, moving about with graceful perfection, a godlike man alone, practicing until he reached the point of exhaustion for the sole satisfaction of knowing that his great skills would never fade. On the court the lawyer was an artist, and the fat man could think of no higher way to praise him.

For his part, the lawyer often had to admit, "Friend fat man, you're no slouch either." For the lawyer lacked the necessary skill to be a master of accurate shooting. The fat man definitely did not; he could make a basket from any point in his half of the court. Many times the lawyer was amazed at the fat man's effortless hook shot; it was as if the ball floated from his hand to the basket (but of course, it did not, for the demon took care to see that they played strictly by mere man rules). The fat man beamed with pleasure every time the net flipped over and hung itself on the rim; toward the end of the game the net was hung up after each goal, and the demon had to exert mental effort to make it unwrap itself. The lawyer was also amazed and the fat man's skills did not lessen as the game progressed. Although the fat man found it more and more difficult to lumber down the court, although he tired rapidly and sweated profusely, his arms and eyes never failed him; when he shot a goal, they had an existence seemingly separate from the rest of his body.

The furry balls were puzzled at what they saw; they wondered why those two strange creatures were running back and forth, what purpose there was in hurling the round object through the hoop, and why the demon sometimes made that shrill noise through the metal object in his beak and pointed an accusing finger at one of the creatures. Not counting elections, their culture had no games, for to have won a game would have relieved the boredom they held so sacred; there was no way for even the most intelligent to comprehend or to guess the purpose of a game, for having hid their intelligence for nearly all their lives, they had forgotten how to use it.

The furry balls suffered a form of future shock; their senses were bombarded with meaningless sounds, meaningless actions; the order of their lives crumbled.

They shivered in their seats; the notion of sitting, of not swimming, was also alien and confusing. They did know one thing: the event they were witnessing could not be ignored on the morrow. Their legends had taught them that their lives could be controlled, that they could influence their environment for the better if they cooperated. Suddenly their legends had been dated; without warning they fully perceived and experienced the true chaos of life they feared so much. They had to discuss and divine some meaning from the chaos, or they would go certifiably insane. They had no choice but to go through the agony of adjusting to one event happening right after another.

The demon blew his whistle louder than he ever had before; the great game was over. The lawyer had won by ten points. He grabbed the basketball and raced up and down the court to illustrate his unbounded joy; he dribbled the ball between his legs, passed the ball from hand to hand, and once he spun about, sliding until he almost fell, but somehow not losing control of the basketball for an instant. "See there, fat man? See there? Huh? Huh? I told you I would win! I told you!"

"I do not recall you making that statement," said the fat man coldly. "In fact, I recall you being rather worried." He sent his sweat and his basketball uniform to the anti-matter universe and replaced the latter with his usual white suit and Borsalino.

The lawyer's basketball uniform also disappeared; his black suit reappeared; he twirled his sword-cane. "Let's see who the gunsel likes now. I'll show you how faithful fans are."

From a place no one could pinpoint a voice shouted, "That's all right, fat man! You'll get him next time!"

The lawyer was crestfallen and speechless. The fat man smiled and patted him on the shoulder. "Do not worry, friend lawyer," he said. "But you must remember, even faithful fans can sometimes be faithful."

"I'll remember that in the future."

The fat man turned to the demon. "And you, my dear friend, did a simply magnificent job of refereeing! It was marvelous! The more I think of it, the more marvelous it becomes!" His voice lowered and lost much of its enthusiasm. "However, I do have one question concerning that personel foul you accused me of toward the end of the third quarter."

"I never discuss a call. It's demeaning." The demon looked away.

The fat man realized that he was not going to get the demon to admit the possibility of an error on his point; there were times when he wished they were not so much alike. He turned his attention to the furry balls, who, having decided that their initiation into chaos was over, were swimming back to their fiery homes. The fat man snapped his fingers, and they were once again in their seats. They had lost all desire to move.

"Thank you, thank you," said the fat man, "for remaining to listen to the after-game speech. I promise that the speech will be brief; I know you must have many things to do. In fact, the speech will consist of one question: where are the bems? You do not know how much that answer means to me and my friends. Why, I wish I had the time to tell you a fraction of the sickness, the poverty, and the hate we have suffered to come this far in our quest for the bems. We *must* have an answer!" His eyes sparkled. "If we do not receive an answer . . . well, allow me to phrase it this way: my pride has been stung because of my defeat at the hands of the lawyer, and I am considering a rematch."

Suddenly the leader of the furry balls cried out, "No! No! I can't take it any longer! Stop! Stop! I can't stand it!"

"You do not have to emote," said the fat man. "You just have to tell us what we want to know."

"Our legends tell us of the bems," said the furry ball. "They're a most foul, despicable race; they're against all the virtues we stand for. You deserve each other because of the crime you've committed against us this day!"

The lawyer raised an eyebrow. "We didn't commit a crime; we only gave an exhibition of what'll happen to you if you don't talk. Now talk, you spineless nits!"

The leader of the furry balls gave the trio the location of the world their legends had told them was the home of the bems.

Bowing, the fat man politely thanked the furry ball; then the trio blinked away. The bleachers and the basketball court disappeared. The furry balls stared at each other without moving; they wondered what was going to happen next.

8. The home world of the bems did not have a name; the bems could not decide which name they liked best. For a long while they wanted to call their native world Snarf. Many bems loved to wander about aimlessly pronouncing the word; they said the word conjured visions of loveliness, that it held many meanings, that a more perfect sound could not be devised. Indeed, many tried to invent a more eloquent name than Snarf, and just when they thought they were close to success, someone near them would simply say, "Snarf," and they realized that their new sound was savage and unsophisticated compared to the sheer poetry of —"Snarf." Imagine their surprise when they had discovered, eons before, that Snarf had already been taken by the dancing fish. For a time there was talk of revenge, but then the bems decided that it was not worth the trouble and they forgot all about naming their world.

Dwit thought of the word Snarf while leaning on a boulder of gold. Each time he mouthed the word, he imagined himself standing in the black emptiness of space with only his innate glory for company, fighting back the terrific onslaught of order in the universe. It was a comical sight, even in his imagination.

A meter and a half tall, he bore a superficial resemblance to a godlike man; he wore platinum-rimmed glasses, a glowing yellow loafer, a glowing blue loafer, red socks, a green ruffled shirt, and a tuxedo with rhinestones in the back forming a pattern of his best profile; he disliked it when people saw his straight back and perfect posture and still did not know who he was. His curly red hair had been thinning for eons; it was short on the top but curled over his ears and hung over his collar. His pale neck was reddened at spots where he was cursed with ingrown hairs. His thin body and oval face made him resemble a fleshed-out stick drawing; all the parts did not seem to fit together. Dwit looked as if he were uncoordinated, but he was actually quite graceful; he was famous for being able to leap into the air, flip his feet, and kick both loafers, spinning high at once, without the aid of thought to achieve the miraculous deed of physical virtuosity.

He smiled; he imagined someone looking at his smile; invariably people laughed at his smile, and so he imagined someone laughing at it. Lately he had been of the opinion that the one thing which could successfully defeat order was laughter, because laughter was always caused by something unexpected and seemingly harmless. He knew that the opinion was only part of the truth, but he was tired of being serious.

He put aside his thoughts of Snarf and watched the landscape change before him.

A tree shrank and shrank until it became a seed, and then the seed disappeared.

A slimy little creature with a green mustache fired his huge pistol at a rock; the rock fired back and nothing was left of the little creature but a wisp of smoke, which said, "Gosh darn it! He did it again!"

A flower spat up.

The fabric of the sky ripped open and Dwit caught a glimpse of the anti-matter universe; he closed the sky before he was sucked into that universe; he had been there on his honeymoon, and the entire experience had not been entertaining enough for a bem with his tastes.

A mountain exploded, and Dwit was covered by ice cream; it was lemon sherbet, which he hated, so he refused to eat it. He turned the ice cream into anchovies, which he loved.

In the distance some of his friends swam in lava; how they could stand it without their suntan lotion, Dwit did not know.

Surrounding themselves with flashing colors, the demon, the lawyer, and the fat man appeared in front of Dwit.

Making himself more comfortable by putting his hands behind his head, Dwit prepared to take a nap. Closing his eyes, he decided that his boring visitors had inferiority complexes.

9. "Good day," said the fat man. "I trust you are a bem."

"My father didn't call me that very often, but nevertheless I've always taken it for granted that I am."

The lawyer said, "We've come a long way to see you."

"And for that you should get a reward," said Dwit, opening his eyes and conjuring a cigar into the lawyer's mouth.

The lawyer was surprised and grateful, even though he normally disliked cigars. He rolled the cigar in his fingers, then put it back into his mouth and made it light itself. As he puffed the cigar he conjured a chair which slowly sank into the mud. He remained stationary in the air. "Thank you. It's not bad, not bad at all. Cherry flavored tobacco?"

"Cherry flavored *chewing* tobacco," said Dwit, closing his eyes and crossing his legs.

"Really?" The lawyer took the cigar from his mouth and stared at it. "I never would have guessed that the flavor would be so exquisite." In reality, the lawyer hated the cigar; he wanted to gag. But he believed the only way they would convince the bems to help them was to fawn over every little favor they received during their visit to the nameless planet. The lawyer turned away as he again puffed on the cigar, so no one would see him turn pale. He watched two flies duel with tiny broadswords.

"The flavor won't be as exquisite as the nap I'm going to take now," said Dwit. "If you three would excuse me. . . ."

The trio was silent for a few minutes; they watched Dwit sleeping.

"Shall I begin?" asked the fat man.

"Begin what?" asked the lawyer.

The demon snatched the dueling flies out of the air with his tongue and ate them, crunching the broadswords. "I'm not ready for it. But I will be if I begin it myself."

"A magnificent idea," said the fat man. "Begin."

"Begin what?" asked the lawyer again.

The demon floated over the sleeping bem. He dropped a pebble on his head.

When the pebble saw what had happened, it became frightened and ran away.

"You'll not sleep until we're finished with you," said the demon. He paused, licking his beak, and then added, "Shorty."

Dwit rubbed his eyes and sat up. He looked about, trying to discover who had been speaking to him. He ignored the lawyer and the fat man, for he had heard them speak and the offending voice had been different. When he was through looking about, he looked up; he saw the demon's huge penis dangling over him. "You wouldn't dare do what I think you might dare do."

"No one has ever given my precious bodily fluids an inspection before. Sometimes, in the dead of night, I get worried about them. What if I excrete blood? I like blood, just like anybody else, but only when it's splattered in the right places. Will I suddenly have painful headaches which will make me a shadow of my former satanic self? Someone really should inspect my precious bodily fluids to see if I'm healthy."

Being careful not to touch the demon's penis, Dwit stood up and walked to safety. "Do you know how long it's been since someone's talked to me that way?"

"Through a beak?" asked the demon. "I'd have guessed that it had never happened before."

The lawyer could not keep his eyes from widening. He touched the fat man's arm hoping that his obese friend would give him an indication that the demon knew what he was doing. But the fat man stood with his hands in his pockets, as if he were watching two obtuse politicians engaged in an abstract discussion. The lawyer did not want anyone to know that he was upset; he tried to act as calm as the fat man. But the fears surging through him were too much to bear; the thought that the provoked bem could take away his godlike abilities without effort would not allow him even the appearance of self-confidence. His anxiety manifested itself in his every hurried gesture, his every noisy breath, his every hesitant word. He inhaled his cigar violently, took it from his mouth when he felt sick to his stomach, and put the cigar back in his mouth when he felt better. He yelped. He had put the cigar in the wrong way. Embarassed at the fat man's rumbling chuckles, directed toward his ineptitude, the lawyer corrected the unfortunate situation and healed his tongue.

The fat man lumbered to Dwit and slapped him on the back. Dwit flew forward into a pile of chartreuse mud, which was ticklish and laughed until Dwit crawled out. The fat man said, "You are certainly a fair-to-middling sport, my friend. You are such a fair-to-middling sport that I would challenge you to a game of basketball had I not already played a game today. You are probably wondering the reasons behind the demon's actions and remarks."

Dwit shooed away the mud on his clothes and rubbed his curly red hair. "No. I'm wondering why I'm letting you get away with this."

"The reason is simple," said the fat man.

"So simple that I'm surprised you haven't guessed the answer already," said the demon, fondling his penis. "Of course, the lawyer's another matter."

"Why am I another matter?" asked the lawyer. *"I'm tired of being another matter.* Why can't I accidently conform every once in awhile, just to give myself a sense of security?"

"You're another matter because you've trained yourself to examine everything as if it were complicated," said the demon.

"It is not a bad trait," said the fat man. "Sometimes it is a valuable one."

"You sad that to make me feel secure," said the lawyer. "You two always say things to make me feel secure. I've been the demon's constant companion for eons, and I've stuck by you both throughout this adventure, despite my cowardly better judgment, and yet I wonder sometimes if you really like me."

"And there's the proof of what I've just said," replied the demon. "A simple godlike man takes a compliment as a compliment; you didn't take the fat man's compliment as a compliment, but as something more. It was, however, only a compliment."

The lawyer smiled and twirled his sword-cane, which in the unusual atmosphere of the bem's planet sparkled green and blue. "Really?"

"Really," said the fat man. "We like you a lot."

"But what's all this have to do with me?" asked Dwit, screaming at the top of his voice. Some of his sound waves turned yellow as they emerged from his mouth.

162

"Don't you know the answer?" asked the demon.

"No."

"It has nothing to do with you," said the demon. "We were sidetracked for a moment."

"We thought that you, of all the beings in the universe, would appreciate something nonsensical," said the fat man.

"I appreciate it all right," said Dwit, kicking a rock into the rainbow stratosphere. "Now why don't you explain the reasons behind your barbaric actions?"

The fat man made several noises by pressing his tongue against the roof of his mouth; clearly, he was disappointed. "Explanations, explanations, everyone wants explanations. Can they not appreciate us without explanations?"

"Apparently not," said the demon, turning his head around so he could watch the mountain which had exploded earlier put itself together, ice cream and all. "I suppose we must explain to him that we were merely testing him."

"Testing me?" asked Dwit, stunned.

"Testing him?" asked the lawyer, confused again.

"To see if your press was accurate," said the fat man. "We had to know if a bem was everything we had heard he was. We wanted to know if a bem had self-control, confidence, a ready wit, and an incredible amount of power. Not a short order, you must understand." He looked at the ground and sighed. "It obviously was too much to expect."

The lawyer slapped his forehead. "In the name of my holy mother! Don't you remember what he can do to us? I don't have to tell you how frightened I am!"

"No, you don't have to tell us," said the demon.

The fat man continued as if the lawyer had not interrupted him. "We needed to know because we have come humbly seeking your aid. Long ago one of your kind altered mere man into godlike man. The time for change has come once again, as it always must."

"Is *that* all?" asked Dwit. "Do you mean to tell me that the preliminaries to the explanation were longer than the explanation itself?"

"We mean to tell you that," said the demon.

"Why?" asked Dwit, before the lawyer could.

"It pleases us to work that way," answered the fat man.

Dwit suddenly smiled; the smile came to him before he realized that the entire incident had amused him. As a true

163

intellectual, he had not played the fool for eons. He had forgotten what a good feeling it was, to do what came naturally without regard for the consequences. One could play the fool without stinging one's pride only in the presence of true comrades. These godlike men were different from what he had expected them to be; they were indeed interesting, almost equal to himself. "I'll help you," he said, "if a friend of mine consents to join me."

Another bem popped out of nowhere. He was Xit. He wore thick glasses, a white t-shirt, green pants, loafers, and a CPA's green plastic eye shade. He had short brown hair and a rectangular face which seemed to be all cheek and forehead, small brown eyes, a tiny mouth capable of enlarging into a wide grin, and a turned-up nose. He appeared to be frightfully common, but his ordinary guise concealed a mind as humorous and as imaginative as Dwit's . . . though not quite as intellectual, Dwit always hastened to add. His pet pig popped into his hands as he said, "I've arrived! A friend of these godlike men known as the gunsel tried to scare me. It was a magnificent, but inherently foolhardy attempt. I liked it a lot. I asked him what he wanted of me, and he said he wanted me here. I asked him why he had tried to scare me, and he said he always worked that way. You must be the fat man. Well, I like your gunsel. You've a good godlike man working for you."

"Thank you."

Changing the subject (for no particular reason), and not doing a very subtle job of it, the lawyer said, "You two don't use your powers much, do you?"

Looking at each other in confusion, Dwit and Xit shrugged. "We use them all the time," Dwit said.

"Get to the point," said Xit.

Looking at each other, the demon and the fat man shrugged. The demon watched the sky turn green; the fat man held his hand over his mouth so the lawyer would not notice him smiling.

"The point is that convincing you to help us was too easy," said the lawyer. "I haven't seen either of you use your powers to do something I couldn't do. I'm wondering if you're really bems."

"Not only am I a bem," said Dwit radiating a musk-scented umbrage, "but I'm also an intellectual."

"After you've been in his company for a time," said Xit, "you'll find that being an intellectual is all he can think about. He also tells a lot of boring stories about his brothers."

"Oh yeah? Do you want me to tell them about your sister?" Dwit retaliated, intellectually.

"I've already seen those pictures," said Xit, rubbing his pig's head. Then, still fascinated by the lawyer's thoroughly inept subject-changing, he decided to see if he could get away with a similar affront. "My pig's name is Sluggy. An unusual name for one of her sex, no?"

"Definitely no," said the lawyer. "I hate pigs. And I also hate people who call themselves bems, but really aren't."

Xit rolled his eyes. "You seem intent upon paying the price of your folly! What would you say if I made this pig as intelligent as you?"

The lawyer stepped backward, almost slipping in mud as he attempted to escape the bem's growing wrath. "You wouldn't dare."

"Watch me." Xit tapped the pig's head.

Strangely colored lights flashed; everyone was blinded.

"Ah, you just did that for the effect," said Dwit.

"It was nevertheless an aesthetic experience. Wasn't it?" Dwit shrugged. "I suppose."

The three godlike men were not debating the positive and negative points of the light show; they were marveling over the sight of a pig suddenly blessed with intelligence. They were also trying to regain their eyesight.

Sluggy wore a red dress with white polka dots, red high-heeled shoes, and black stockings. She sported false eyelashes and a generous amount of lipstick and rouge. She shifted her cigarette in a long black plastic holder from one side of her mouth to the other and said to the lawyer, "I think I love you, big boy. Whatcha doing tonight? Nothing interesting, I hope, because I'm sure I can think of something interesting for you to do."

The lawyer held up his hands, as if the gesture could ward off Sluggy's verbal advances. "Oh no! Not to me! I'm nothing if I'm not true to my true love, whether she's true to me or not. I'm leaving this place. When you join me with the bems, my friends, make sure you leave *that* right here where it belongs."

165

The lawyer blinked away; he was relieved to be speeding to Earth, although the infinite blackness of space made him uncomfortable when he was alone.

10. The godlike men, waking early one morning, found themselves thinking that there had been few pleasant surprises in their lives lately. They found themselves with the deisre for a few more hours' sleep; when they awoke, at last, it was invariably near noon, with less of the day before them.

This morning, however, their anxieties did not pass away; with them also came a sense of *déjà vu*. The anxieties were pleasant; no one was worried.

When they looked out their windows they saw once again the skywriter flying his Fokker triplane and indulging in his favorite hobby.He wrote:

YOUR LIVES WILL BE DELIGHTFULLY ALTERED BY
THE**NEW** **IMPROVED**

FAIR
PRESENTED BY
THOSE WILD, WHACKY, AND WONDERFUL BEMS
DWIT AND XIT

The good word spread fast. Soon the entire population wondered how their lives would be delightfully altered. (Several godlike men barely remembered a time when someone else had tried to alter their lives at a fair, but the alteration was not to have been a delightful one. A few godlike men tried to remember the details, but they did not try very hard; there was so much future to look forward to, there was no time to spend dwelling in the past.)

All godlike men went about their self-appointed tasks with renewed vigor. Even thinking clean the dishes assumed a less practical, more mystical meaning. For eons everyone had *believed* that life was good and that it could only get better; at last, it *was* about to get better. Godlike men whistled tunelessly as they walked down the streets; they waved at eternal children who, instead of jeering and throwing

166

melting ice cream, waved back. Godlike women paused to hear the birds sing "Anything Goes" and "Kiss Me, Kate." The songs seemed much more intricate now that life was going to change for the better; the singing seemed more reflective, happier, with deeper emotional significance. People saluted the sun for doing such a good job. They thought that perhaps they should create more apartment complexes and then, when they got around to it, they should bring more godlike children into the world, real children, for a change of pace, real children who would benefit because they had been raised in a happy time.

Petty rivalries were momentarily forgotten. The shrink drank a cup of coffee with his competitors. The Queen of England who called herself a virgin drank a toast to her older sister. The writer with the trenches around his castle loaded his machine guns with blanks. The racing driver forgot to hoard oil. The green worm with glasses played double solitaire with the Big Red Cheese (and let him win every game). Petty friendships became important friendships. The poet who yearned for childhood did not say "Fooey" when a casual acquaintance expressed admiration for one of his poems. The model airplane builder discussed the fine art of applying glue with the model car builder, who in turn discussed the same subject with the model motorcycle builder. And when the model motorcycle builder wanted to relate his discovery of a particular nuance of glue application, the model airplane builder listened attentively, although he had heard it before. Important friendships became relaxed; people were actually glad to see their close friends. When the priest spoke to the professional layman on the street, he did not say, "I trust you have found the numerous blessings of salvation and that you will pray twice as long tonight," but said instead, "Hey, buddy, what's the rap? Good to see you! How's the little woman?" Then the priest told the professional layman a dirty joke he had heard from the bald priest dressed in blood red robes.

The next day godlike mankind became even happier, even more at peace with itself when Dwit and Xit gave their advertising campaign an auspicious debut. They paraded down the golden streets of several golden cities, and the people applauded their parading. The people applauded their parading not because they marched in step, but be-

167

cause they rode on hippos who cakewalked in step. Dwit and Xit sat side-saddle with their legs crossed. They plucked at their banjos and sang:

> *If you're looking for a fair, go see Dwit,*
> *If you're looking for fun, go see Xit,*
> *Go see Dwit, go see Xit.*
> *You'll get better rides with Dwit,*
> *You'll get better deals with Xit,*
> *So if you're looking for a fair,*
> *Go see Dwit and Xit, go see Dwit and Xit,*
> *Go see Dwit and Xit, go see Dwit and Xit,*
> *Yeah!*

The race of godlike men loved it. They gave Dwit, Xit, and the marching hippos a standing ovation. At the conclusion of their commercial, Dwit and Xit bowed and thanked the people. The people wondered what they were going to do next; they knew that if the fair was only half as good as their commercials, it would be well worth attending.

The following day Dwit and Xit rode winged broncos. The day after they rode giraffes. And then brontosauri, kangeroos, alligators, giant rabbits, and pterodactyls. Finally they rode a pink grizzly bear and called it their dog Spot. Godlike mankind loved that ploy most of all. In each city after Dwit and Xit had finished their song, the people cried, "Speech! Speech! We must have a speech! Give us a sales pitch we can't resist! Give us a sales pitch we won't forget!"

Dwit stood up on his dog Spot, wiped the fog from his glasses so he could see, and said, "You know, my dog Spot's a good old dog. The dog food I give him every day is all meat, and he likes it. He eats it all."

The people were delighted with Dwit's sense of humor. They demanded more.

Dwit said, "You know, speaking of my dog, Spot, we've got a great fair for you. It's not just a fair fair; it's *quite* a fair. As a true intellectual, I can tell you that it's fun to have fun at a fair without thinking deep thoughts or wondering about the futility of it all. In fact, we have a fair for you that you won't forget. If you think you've forgotten the last fair you went to, you certainly won't forget this one. It won't even cost you some fame and glory to get in. To get in you just walk in. How about that, folks? So why don't you all just come down to this fair when it opens? Have we got a great time for you!"

The people cheered and demanded that Xit also make a speech. When Xit stood up on his dog Spot, Dwit whispered, "Let's see if you can top that one! No one can talk like a common godlike man the way a true intellectual can when he puts his mind to it."

Xit ignored his friend and said, "Hi, people. Xit the bem here. Let's talk about being carefree, let's talk about fun, let's talk about the fair! You know, some people like my dog Spot can't appreciate a good fair the way you can, and I can say this because I'm not a true intellectual like my friend here, but only a false intellectual. And all us false intellectuals don't have a thought about the futility of it all when we're having fun. Well, this fair's gonna be a true bargain, and you're gonna be the ones who're gonna walk away with all the good deals. We got so much fun at this fair that we're just dying to get rid of it. In fact, we're so overstocked on fun that we can't stop smiling, not even for an instant. So why don't y'all come down and see our fair when it opens? Have we got a great time for *you!*"

The people liked that speech more than they liked Dwit's. They demanded more and more commercials. In each golden city the bems had to tell the people that they had a tight schedule to adhere to, and that everyone would have to wait until the fair if they wanted to get more. Everyone said they would be at the fair.

And in each golden city, standing at the outermost edges of the crowds were the demon, the lawyer, and the fat man. (The gunsel was always nearby, sometimes lingering in the crowd, sometimes looking at the proceedings from a rooftop.)

It was a whirlwind tour they were making, and they would have enjoyed it immensely had they not written Dwit and Xit's speeches (the bems knew next to nothing about advertising, despite their great knowledge and power).

"I wish I hadn't written Xit's speech so well," said the lawyer, near the tour's end. "Then I could criticize it. As things are, the speech is, well, perfect."

"Only because I corrected the grammar," said the demon, picking lint from his naval. "Line-editing your copy is pure agony."

"And because I convinced him that he should write down to the masses so that all would understand Xit," said the fat man. "I gave him a complete set of guidelines."

"But the genius was mine," said the lawyer. "I'm an artist!" He twirled his sword-cane. He strutted about in a little circle, then suddenly stopped short. He ceased twirling his sword-cane and looked at the demon and the fat man, who knew that something had occurred to him because of his confused expression. "I wish I knew one thing."

The demon solemnly stroked his beak. "I know. I've often wondered about that myself."

The crowd began to break up; people pushed themselves past the trio; the trio ignored the people. The fat man said, "Indeed, I, too, have the same question on my mind. We have seen to all the details of the fair, but we do not know how Dwit and Xit plan to depress the race of godlike mankind."

11. The big day finally came. Although it was actually the second big day of its kind, no one seemed to care. The entire population was there, including the godlike men who usually missed such affairs because their identities dictated that they be iconoclastic. No one was disappointed; the fair was three times better than its commercials.

The snang with the talking fingers was a main attraction. Snangs were retarded ferns with feet and hands, but with no legs or arms, from a planet near Snarf. A snang was usually a confused beast because each of its ten fingers contained a little head, complete with eyes, noses, ears, brains, and mouths; each finger was a separate entity. The snang could embark upon a certain course of action only when a majority of fingers deemed it proper; a tie among the fingers meant that the snang would be indecisive until the tie was broken. This state was bearable for snangs who had a finger which was a natural-born leader, but those snangs were always dull. The fat man had selected for the fair a snang with six male fingers and four female fingers.

Consequently most of the fingers' thoughts centered upon who nestled with whom. Two male fingers lusted after the affections of a certain dizzy female finger who was hardly worth the trouble, and another female finger who *was* worth the trouble had succeeded in hopelessly complicating the situation by flirting with three male fingers, making each male believe that she was his.

The eternal children loved to watch the snang standing in the middle of the stage. Its fingers crawled over one another, screaming, biting, insulting, and sometimes loving. Instinctively the snang tried to walk across the stage toward the pool of water the fat man had placed there. Although each entity was thirsty, the fingers cared more about their internal politics than their survival. The snang quivered when it scooted forward, and finally it fell flat, near death; and still the fingers argued about who had the better reason to love whom.

"Symbolic, is it not?" asked the fat man.

No one knew the answer. They were too busy laughing to care.

Another attraction was the skull with the black sense of humor. The skull rested on a Morris chair and told one-liners to the crowd. When no one laughed it said in a halting voice, "A good 'un, huh? Huh? Didn't you think it was a good 'un?" Then everyone laughed.

The race of godlike man also saw a creature who could not maintain its shape. No one knew what kind of shape the creature would have liked best, least of all the creature itself. Usually it was able to remain suspended above the stage, so when it tried to form a shape by shoving part of its globby mass downward, it would uncontrollably flatten out and snap into its undefined form, its parts shooting haphazardly in all directions. This event happened three times, and each time the audience laughed and laughed; they called it a great innovation in slapstick, and many wished they had creatures like that in their homes so they could watch them early in the morning and late at night.

The creature who could not maintain its shape tried several ploys to arrive at a stable shape; the one it used most frequently was to color itself and puff its body so it would appear to be covered with fur, or to be pock-marked, or to be clothed. Each time it seemed to approach the attainment of the definite form of any being or thing in the universe, the creature lost control and again became a white mass. Once, it obtained the basic shape of a godlike man; the creature spent two hours obtaining legs and trousers and shoes, a torso and arms and legs, and a soft delicate godlike man's face. The audience watched the creature's painful metamorphosis in awe and in silence; not even the cruel eternal children giggled. For a moment it seemed as if the doomed creature would finally be successful, and it glanced about in triumph. But as it took its first step, placing most of its weight on one leg, its body slid down the leg and the creature plopped on the stage.

The audience howled. The audience felt the creature would surely give up. However, even as the audience applauded the good show and stood up to leave the creature floated again, and its body gyrated once more. The audience found its resolve delightful.

A light show spattered the skies in a chaos of color (as Dwit and Xit put it). As the godlike men and women and their eternal children wandered from show to show, from ride to ride, from concession stand to concession stand, they glanced up and saw the gobs of red rolling like lava, merging with gobs of yellow and blue, creating hundreds of colors. Black and white rolled through the sky, and the colors sometimes lightened and darkened in a hypnotic pattern which no one could discern, though people spent long minutes trying.

People found themselves mysteriously compelled to fasten their attention on one bubble of color, watching it float across the sky, being pushed by other bubbles, going up and down, until it finally broke apart into tinier bubbles which in turn floated across the sky, or merged into other bubbles and formed new colors. The race of godlike man found itself feeling that the universe was breaking apart.

They felt they were standing among huge chunks of that intangible essence of life which made them intuit that all aspects of their destiny, even their most inconsequential games, were important.

Yeh they felt so small at the same time; it was damaging to their egos to feel small, but they did not mind because the bittersweet notion was new to them and, sometimes, comforting. Many conjectured that if such a feeling remained they would come to realize that their mistakes and personal failings were unimportant in the vastness of the universe; others conjectured not at all.

Because of the light show, the godlike men felt everything they had ever felt. Such an experience did not make them feel humble, despite the accompanying sensation of smallness, but it did make them feel a tenderness toward the concept of life in general, a fleeting instant of compassion which they lost when they went inside a tent to see an attraction. Several godlike men remembered forgotten hopes and aspirations, schemes and ideas which they might have had buried in their collective unconscious since they had been mere mortals; they resolved that soon, possibly tomorrow, they would take stock of their lives and try to change their direction.

But that too was the sensation of an instant.

For the most part, the light show made everyone happy, and the entire race would have watched it all day and all night had there not been so much more to see.

And there were hundreds of other attractions which the race of godlike men could not help but marvel at. The dancing fish from Snarf were there, and so were the Ebony Kings, strutting across their stage. All the old favorite rides were there—the ferris wheel spinning through complex configurations of time; the octopus that was a real live giant octopus; the candy spaceships. Godlike mankind was dazzled and amazed at the incredible imagination shown by Dwit and Xit; the bems were the best thing that had ever happened on Earth.

Of course, no one knew that the demon, the lawyer, and the fat man had a hand in the fair, too; had they known, they might have suspected a plot and elected to ignore the fair. Nor did they know that the gunsel was carefully watching them. He would signal the fat man when the time was right to depress the race of godlike man.

All involved in the plot were satisfied. There had been no underlying concept behind the first fair; the demon, the lawyer, and the fat man had expected the crawling bird to do all their work for them. In this fair the light show, the creature who could not maintain its shape, and several other attractions were calculated to put the race unknowingly in the proper frame of mind to be depressed.

173

12. The gunsel signaled the fat man.

The light show in the sky flashed on and off; godlike mankind knew at once that the time had come for the mysterious big attraction, the one Dwit and Xit had promised would delightfully alter them. By now no one was worried or anxious. Since the change was to be for the better, there obviously was nothing to be worried about.

Godlike mankind filed inside the auditorium; each person tried to sit as close to the front as possible; no one tried to find several empty seats in a row so all of his group could sit together; it was every godlike man for himself.

Of course, some did not have to worry if they came in late. The Queen of England who called herself a virgin walked straight to the front row, leaving her royal entourage behind. The demon and the fat man would not have noticed had not the lawyer jabbed them both in the side and pointed at her. The demon and the fat man nodded solemnly as they watched her tap the Big Red Cheese on the shoulder and asked him to give up his seat. The Big Red Cheese looked around while wondering what to do. Since everyone expected him to give up graciously his good view of the stage for the godlike lady, he did.

The lawyer snickered. "That'll show him." Then his expression sobered. "Kitty isn't with him." He stood up and looked around the auditorium. "I don't see her. I wonder where she is."

"She's here. No doubt about it," said the demon, turning his head three hundred and sixty degrees.

"And no doubt with someone else," said the fat man.

"That's good," said the lawyer. "It means that the Big Red Cheese is suffering right now."

"Not as much as he's going to," said the demon.

"That's funny," said the lawyer. "I don't see the gunsel either."

"He is here," said the fat man, chuckling. "A godlike man like the gunsel is seen only when he wants to be seen."

"And everyone can see you, friend lawyer," said the demon. "Sit down and relax. Depression is imminent."

174

The lawyer flopped into his seat, crossed his legs, and sulked. "I know, I know. I just wish I knew who Kitty's with, that's all."

"What difference does it make?" asked the fat man. "You would just hate him, too."

"I know, I know," said the lawyer. "I hate him already. But what's the fun in hating someone if you don't know who he is?"

"Gee, I wished I'd asked that," said the demon.

Further conversation was terminated by the dimming of the lights. Soon the race of godlike man was bathed in darkness.

A spotlight flashed on; Dwit and Xit danced to center stage. The bems were greeted with deafening applause. Before the final show had even begun, people shouted, "More! More!" as if all they had hoped for was a final glimpse of the bems. Dwit and Xit bowed and waved to the audience several times before they asked for quiet. Twenty minutes later godlike mankind was silent. Dwit and Xit looked at each other and smiled as if they were already seasoned entertainers who could do no wrong, who held all audiences in the palms of their hands.

"We coached them well," whispered an excited lawyer to the fat man.

The fat man poked the lawyer in the side, a clever ploy that told the lawyer the fat man desired him to be silent until the show was over. The lawyer was silent, but not because he respected the fat man's wishes; the lawyer was in pain.

Dwit stepped forward and said, "Good evening, friends. No, our dog Spot isn't with us tonight. We sent him home to the forest to take care of his business. And you ought to see his business expenses sometime."

"That was a good one," said Xit, after the laughter had peaked. "May I use it at our next show?"

"Only a true intellectual such as myself can say something like that and get away with it," replied Dwit. He turned to the audience. "A lot of you are probably wondering why I called this meeting. Indeed, I was wondering myself until Xit told me. And furthermore, a lot of you are probably wondering just why Xit and I have come to your lovely planet here. I could tell you why just by showing you three of your most illustrious citizens, but that'll have to wait until later. Right now, however, Xit and I must show you something. As promised, it will delightfully alter your lives."

Xit snapped his fingers.

The universe dropped away beneath the race of godlike man.

Each godlike man floated alone in an infinite black void. The void was not space; there were no stars, no planets, no distant destinations providing the hope of warmth, rest, and direction. Each godlike man felt as if he were spinning about, but he did not know for sure due to the lack of direction. Each godlike man tried to close his eyes, as if to exchange an unknown blackness for a known blackness. Closing eyes did not help. There was still the awareness of being alone: loveless in the infinite void.

The fact that eventually all godlike men would forever have to face such a cold, unending blackness thundered in on them with only the banal hope that perhaps the memory of having done something worthwhile during life might provide comfort throughout an existence of total despair.

Suddenly memory was snatched from each godlike man, and when memory left, so did hope. Each godlike man felt that he had been floating in the void forever; his past stretched behind him; and he could remember no birth; there was no concept of death. Each godlike man wondered if his only purpose in life was to search for an identity in a place where there was no identity to be found.

The answer was simple: *that* was his *only* purpose.

With no distractions or memory, with what abstract thoughts he could summon, each godlike man felt smaller, more useless than he ever had before. Each godlike man believed that he saw reality for the first time; he learned his true place in the universe. There was no pleasure in the learning, as those few had found pleasure in the learning while watching the light show spatter color against the skies of Earth; there was only pain! Pain that throbbed inside each godlike man's stomach like the death of a friend.

Memory returned, but the hope of forgetfulness did not; although each godlike man wanted to ignore the facts, he could not. Each godlike man decided that if he ever escaped from the void, he would elect to forget the facts. But how would he escape? How could he forget a lesson he had learned so thoroughly?

The questions were too much to ponder; the answers were too obvious. Each godlike man decided that he should alter his outlook on his existence. True, his existence appeared to be wretched on the surface, but perhaps if he looked for advantages, he would discover some.

Each godlike man searched.

There was one advantage: order. Each godlike man had the comfort of knowing that nothing unexpected would ever happen to him. Nothing at all would happen during the unending moments of life. In that respect, each godlike man had defeated the chaos that had savaged him.

Each godlike man decided his victory was not worth it. There had to be something more to life. It did not matter what.

A vision, perhaps.

A vision that would enable each godlike man to transcend the void, that would comfort him, that would provide him with the hope of achieving something.

But there were no visions in the void. There was nothing. With one exception there was no longer even the hope of hope. That one exception was the possibility that the void did not represent death itself. Perhaps death, the nullification of all existence, was some other place. If so, death could be reached by the extreme measure of suicide.

Each godlike man willed his life-force to cease to exist.

But each life force lived on.

Each godlike man was overcome by a final wave of despair. Each one wondered how he could go on floating in the void without becoming hopelessly insane. Each godlike man experienced a numbing depression he would never forget. If he escaped from the void and returned to his former existence, then the depression would also return, and he would experience it at the oddest moments, for the strangest reasons.

Of course, that would not stop him from trying to elect to forget it.

Dwit, Xit, the demon, the lawyer, and the fat man knew that each godlike man never would, so they allowed each godlike man to return to his place in the auditorium.

13. People were shocked to have returned so suddenly. They gripped their armrests and looked at the people surrounding them. It was difficult to believe that the void, which had seemed so real, was gone. Because it was so difficult to believe, each godlike man reached out and touched another, but only for an instant.

On the stage Dwit and Xit shook hands. Xit turned to the audience and said, "Well, what did you think of our little exhibition? Pretty good, wasn't it?"

"I liked it," said the demon, floating toward the stage, in front of his friends.

"I knew you would," said Xit. "But what about the rest of you?"

Godlike men whispered to each other, squirmed in their seats, and stared at the floor. No one wanted to be the first to voice a decision. Finally the Queen of England who called herself a virgin stood up with her head held high and proud. "We, for one, have elected to forget it," she said.

Dwit pursed his lips and rubbed his curly red hair. "We, for one, are disappointed. I realized that you would want to try to forget depression as you had before, but I didn't think you would actually be so foolhardy as to try. It's a ridiculous notion. Even if you could forget it, we would just make you remember it again. You'd have to float through the void again. Would you like that?"

The Queen of England who called herself a virgin sat down. She still held her head high and proud, but her voice quivered as she said, "We, for one, have elected to remember it."

"Good dog!" exclaimed the lawyer. When he realized that he had accidently insulted the Queen, he hid behind the fat man. "Maybe she didn't hear it," he mumbled.

"And it is well indeed that you've elected to remember depression," said Dwit. "For to know depression is to know one of the great lessons of life. Depression will force you to become ambitious. It'll give you a new lease on life. It'll force you to have visions of a world without depression, and you'll constantly seek to make those visions a reality."

"Depression will make you more like the demon, the lawyer, and the fat man," said Xit. "Once you confiscated all their fame and glory, you little rascals you. Now you should return it to them; you should give them all the fame and glory there in on this tacky little planet. They're responsible for your depression, and you should love them for it. True, *we* made you depressed, and *we* were the ones who gave you your powers; we changed you from mere man into godlike man. But that was nothing; we just did that for a lark. The demon, the lawyer, and the fat man had a vision, and *that* is what terrifically impressed unimpressionable us. If you follow their example, you might rid yourself of depression some day."

"What about it?" asked Dwit. "Huh? Huh?"

"This is it," said the fat man to the demon and the lawyer. "In a few moments we will know if it was all worthwhile."

"You speak only of the short term," said the demon. "As for the long term . . . well, we must wait until the long term arrives."

The Queen of England pondered the matter. "Perhaps what you say is true. There are some things we have wanted, some godlike men whom we have wanted for a long time. Now we have the urge to get them to ease our depression. And we are too depressed to care about who has all the empty fame and glory. Let them have it!"

The lawyer jumped up, threw his sword-cane into the air, caught it, and shouted, "Hip, hip, hooray! Hip, hip, hooray!" The demon breathed fire. The fat man, brushing lint from his white jacket, strutted about the stage.

His actions were greeted with applause. He held up his hand, asking for silence. When godlike mankind was silent, he said. "Thank you, thank you. I really need that fame and glory; I did not know how much I had missed it. I am grateful that you have received the valuable gift of depression in the proper spirit, for that means that some day our race will become one of the most important in the universe. The time has definitely come for us to leave our puny backyard."

The fat man was greeted with more applause. When the applause died, the fat man spoke to the bems. "What of you? Will you remain with us for a spell?"

Xit said, "No. I had a miserable affair of the heart recently and before I came here to pursue our holy cause, I met the bem who has the ability to ease my own depression."

"I know *her*," said Dwit. "She's *mine*."

"She is not!" said Xit. "She's *mine*! She loves only me!"

"No, she doesn't," said Dwit. "As a true intellectual, I know when a woman *loves* me and *hates* you!"

Still arguing, the bems blinked away, on their long path home.

The fat man turned his attention to the audience; he wanted to make a lengthy speech, to bask in fame and glory as a lizard basks in the sun. "Now I would like to introduce to you the two godlike men who joined me on this quest for depression. . . ."

14. The day following the second fair, the demon created a Gothic castle with gargoyles hunkering on the towers. The castle was made of pitch black stone. Its halls were long and drafty, lit by dim candles spaced a meter apart. The rugs appeared ancient and worn; to look at the frayed ends and the beaten paths, one would not have suspected that the rugs had been newly created. The water in the moat was stagnant and tinged with green; the demon created some especially ugly serpents to live in it. "I had to celebrate," he explained to his friends. "I couldn't waste time taking out the garbage for my landlady. I'm an important godlike man now. In a few years everyone will realize the true worth of what we've done, and we should live in a style commensurate with our fame and glory."

Fondling his penis, he floated inside the castle to inspect the premises, to see if reality lived up to his expectations.

The lawyer could not help but agree with the demon's main points. However, he did not care where he lived; he still cared only for Kitty. He was disappointed to find that she was not at her apartment when he called on her. Not knowing where else to turn, he asked the demon if he could stay in the castle.

"Of course, friend lawyer," said the demon. "The only

180

luxuries are the several Morris chairs I've created. You realize that it would more suit my brooding, satanic image if I lived alone in my decrepit estate, but I realize, in turn, that one with my fame and glory is above such tiny considerations as images. Images. Humph! Of course you can stay."

The lawyer twirled his sword-cane, bowed, and thanked the demon. If one had to be alone, he reasoned, it was best to be alone with a friend.

The fat man found himself in a somewhat worse position. Although the vision of a world with depression had not been initially his, he had lived the vision and had fought for it with all the power and originality he could command. He had lived only for the vision, and that was his problem. In the old days he had worked on many matters at once, and when one matter was done, he could immediately turn his attention to another. But those matters had been insignificant ones, he was ashamed to admit; now he cared only for significant matters. At the moment there were no significant matters for him to turn his attention to. "I would live with my wife," explained the fat man, "for she ignores me no longer. However, she is not an extremely understanding godlike woman. She is too depressed to be good company. And on top of that, she has cultivated a fondness for perverted relationships, and is living with a slimy homosexual in a black suit. I hate to admit it, but the homosexual has talents to equal my own. If I tried to win her back, I would have someone worthy of my mettle to practice on."

"Of course you may stay," said the demon, licking his fingers clean. "Perhaps it would be best if the three of us remained together while we watch godlike mankind do battle with depression. I trust the gunsel will be with us in the castle, too. It'll do my evil soul good to know that an unseen figure is lurking behind me."

"The gunsel will be with us," said the fat man. "There can be no doubt."

"Excellent," said the demon. They shook hands on it.

The trio and the mysterious gunsel retired to the castle, and during the next two weeks they watched the realities of their vision come to pass.

181

SLICES OF LIFE: FIVE

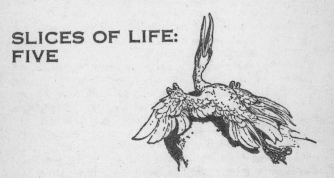

Depression was not such a good thing after all.

The brilliant spectacle of sunrise was no longer heart-warming. The golden sunrays, the soft blue sky, and the white fog were still lovely; each sunrise was still picturesque, beautiful beyond the descriptive powers of even the most erudite godlike man; however, everyone imagined the sunrise to be foreboding, well suited to their disposition. The golden apartment building, the golden sidewalks, and the golden gutters seemed dull and no longer inspired awe in the works of godlike man. Occasionally someone who perceived the truth ventured to remark that the environment should be changed, but no one knew in exactly what way it should be changed. The sunrise could never be made beautiful enough to keep godlike mankind from being depressed, nor could it be made foreboding enough to mirror depression.

Gradually, the early risers slept later and later; people went to bed earlier at night; they wanted the day to be over as soon as possible.

There were no grandiose schemes, no new identities, no reaffirmations of eternal love, no great works of art. There was nothing.

The stand-up comic wandered aimlessly through the golden streets. His eyes were glazed; he found it difficult to sleep at night. As he walked, he did not notice the dirty eternal children sitting on the curbs, tossing pebbles across the street. He was busy, trying to think of a joke that would make people laugh; it was a more difficult task than trying to sleep. Often he was seen grabbing a godlike man by the elbow ad saying, "A godlike man and woman were walking down the street. I forgot the joke." Then he played a few hasty chords on his violin. The squeaking sounds delighted no one, least of all himself.

The two whacky, lovable gangsters discovered that fried chicken was not as good as it used to be. What was the use of robbing a bank of its fame and glory if there was no good fried chicken to celebrate with afterward? The gangsters tried the crunchy fried chicken *once* to see if that would help; it did not help. Throwing up their hands in despair, they decided that they would not rob a bank again until the fried chicken regained its flavor. This did not make the fat southern cop happy; he had always wanted to catch them in the act. He was forced to retire to the rocking chair on his front porch.

The insidious Oriental doctor found that toying with an infernal machine was a useless pastime. If only he could have a machine that was not a toy to play with, but which was a weapon to be wielded. He searched throughout his dungeons, looked through eons' worth of blueprints, and could find nothing. He wondered where his great powers had gone. He sat on his throne and listened to bored lackeys sing praises to him; sometimes he tried to make friends with his son, but that was no good either. The kid was plain surly and kept making vague, chopping movements in the air with the edges of his callused hands.

The poet who yearned for the return of his childhood watched the eternal children play basketball across the street, and he thought of his real daughter, of the idyllic days before she had married the poet who drowned himself daily. He wrote a brief poem about his daughter taking showers after watching boys play basketball; then he took a shower himself.

The frat guy wearing the green turtleneck sweater and sporting the crewcut discovered that his friends had lost their desire to drink beer during the happy hour. Every Friday he sat alone at the bar in the basement with the loud stereo and the flashing red and blue lights. He did not drink his beer; he stared at it until it became warm. He sipped it, found that it was awful, and then poured it down the sink. He poured another glass and stared at it until it, too, became warm.

The rock star had no more messages to impart; all the joy and rebellion in his music was gone. His new songs reminded everyone of what he used to do, and what he used to do had been better. The rock star continued to write, play, and dance across the stage; in his search for a new musical direction, he tried to find another musical genius to worship, a genius who would show him the way. The rock star's music deteriorated and deteriorated.

The galactic hero questioned his overblown sense of honor. He lay awake nights thinking that he had led a narrow life, that there were more important things than fighting enemies. But what was more important than making life safe for others? What was more delightful than the delight he took in making the kill? The galactic hero did not know the answers. He was not equipped to know the answers.

The Big Red Cheese discovered that his carefree existence had been meaningless. Every morning he wondered how he could have spent an eternity totally devoid of significance; every answer was unsatisfactory. Leaping tall buildings in a single bound provided him with no pleasure. Whenever he looked into a mirror, he was afraid that he was ugly, supremely unattractive. He did not believe that any godlike woman would ever want him. And to think that once he had been a great lover!

It was the same for every godlike man on Earth. Every sight was a sad sight. Godlike mankind believed that there was no hope, and so it did not fight the onslaught of depression.

CHAPTER SIX

The demon floated to the barred window and stared at the enormous hailstones plummeting from the angry black clouds. The hailstones cracked and popped against the castle walls. They hurtled between the bars and struck the demon. Still the demon stared at the bleak countryside, with the trees bending under the strength of the cold wind, with the darkness of the sky relieved only by sudden flashes of lightning. The only sign that showed he was not entirely oblivious to the hailstones striking him was that his hands covered his immense penis.

"Well, friend fat man," said the demon, "it appears that we've miscalculated."

The fat man did not answer for a few moments. He looked at himself in a mirror. He reasoned that of all the current sad sights on Earth, the saddest one was himself with crestfallen features. He tried to smile, but did not have the strength or will for it. At least his white suit was clean. Squirming in the Morris chair and making the mirror disappear, he said, "Evidently there was more to mere man than we had hoped. Our race is a defeated one. There is no hope."

The demon floated across the room, near a suit of armor and a coat of arms, and fondled his penis where it could be exposed in safety. "We must do something. We're responsible for this."

"Who cares about responsibility? I, for one, care about nothing. I do not even care about my gunsel. He has given up all hope of effectively shadowing people. They welcome

187

fear as a pleasant diversion from ther usual mental state."

"It would seem to me that fear would be no good for them. Fear's a fleeting emotion."

The fat man crossed his ankles and waved his hand. His gestures were no longer meaningful. "You are correct. My gunsel is spending all his time in the bathroom you have prepared for him. Perhaps he believes he can think of an answer there."

"I don't see how," said the demon, lighting the wood under the caldron in the firepalce; he was preparing himself a bowl of chicken soup.

"It does not matter what my gunsel does," said the fat man.

"You're right. It doesn't matter." Desperately craving the chicken soup, he floated about the room. He blew lightly on the candles to watch the flames flicker. He stared at the titles of his books in the hope that an inspiration would come to him through them. "We must do something."

"You keep saying that."

The demon pricked his finger on his beak and let the black pus drop onto his tongue. "We're sorry characters, aren't we? We've endured setbacks before, and now we don't believe we'll endure this one. Our conversation was once witty, full of sparkling ideas and meaningful insights; now it's dull and uninspired, full of nothing."

"There is nothing to say," said the fat man.

"Unfortunately, that's the exception that proves the rule."

They were silent for nearly half an hour. The only noises were the slurps caused by the demon as he upended the red-hot caldron and drank his chicken soup (the fat man was not hungry). They were silent until the lawyer, dripping wet from an excursion outside, returned and sat in the other Morris chair. He threw his sword-cane on the floor. He did not seem to mind that his black suit was muddy and disarrayed. "Nuts!" he said.

The fat man's eyes widened. "Really! No matter how bad things are, that kind of language is inappropriate!"

"Yes, it is," said the lawyer, hugging his knees to his chest. He did not look at his friends, but at the empty caldron burning its imprint into the wooden table. "I've finally found out where Kitty's staying."

"Oh?" said the demon. "Perhaps there's hope for at least one of us."

"Did you visit her?" asked the fat man.

"Of course, of course. My visit proved there's hope for none of us."

"I take it that the failure of the visit was your doing," said the demon, carefully scratching the small of his back.

"No. I was more debonair than ever. I bathed and shaved; I brushed my teeth; I read the dictionary three times before visiting her. No, the fault was hers, if she can be said to have faults."

"It can be said," replied the demon. "But please tell us what happened."

"I suppose it doesn't matter if you know," said the lawyer, putting his feet on the floor. "She told me that she had indeed discovered I was the only possible love for her."

"That's bad?" asked the demon.

"She also told me that life is worthless. 'There's no point in finding your true love if it gives you no joy.' I tried to change her mind, but she adhered to her course. I couldn't convince her that there's more to life than great pain and suffering. I talked and talked at her; I must have talked for hours. But it was no good. And I felt so sorry for her. I wish that there was something I could have done. When I saw her eyes and how they glistened from her tears, I realized that she was looking to me for hope. And I could do nothing. I tell you, I've never felt so useless and depressed. There's no hope for any of us."

"You should have done *something*," said the demon.

"What?" asked the lawyer.

"*Anything*," said the fat man.

"It doesn't matter what," said the demon.

"What was I supposed to do? She had told me herself that there was nothing I could do. Allow me to repeat: what was I supposed to do? Take her in my arms and kiss her? Make violent love to her? *Force her to be happy?*"

The fat man raised his eyebrows and looked at the demon. The demon fondled his penis with a suddenly discovered excitement, and looked at the fat man. The lawyer looked at them both; there was electricity in the air, and he did not know why.

Suddenly the fat man pointed his finger at the ceiling and screamed, "Friend lawyer, you have hit upon it!"

The fat man lumbered to the lawyer with frightening speed, picked him up from the Morris chair, and held him in a crushing embrace. When the fat man finally dropped the dizzy lawyer, the demon floated behind him and gave him a resounding slap on the back. The lawyer slammed to the floor.

"What did I say?" he asked, looking up. "What did I say?"

The demon did something no one had ever seen him do before. He leaned backward until he hung upside down "Depression is out!" he yelled. "Sexism is in!"

"Sexism?" said the lawyer. "What's that?"

The fat man flopped into a Morris chair. "Sexism was another of mere man's shortcomings, and it was a most basic one. Women were not people; they were bodies to be used for pleasure and for nothing else. Virginity was also important. Can you believe that?"

"No," replied the lawyer. He was still confused.

"Also, while sexism was in vogue, making love became a source of pride to mere man," said the demon. "Men used to gather in locker rooms and talk about what they liked a lot and why they liked to wear their jocks a lot. Men took pride in the fact that they were men, an accident of birth."

"But how does it help us?" asked the lawyer, standing up.

"Sexism creates roles," said the fat man. "The woman lived to be a mother; the man lived to be a father. Godlike mankind needs roles."

"Men were known to spend large amounts of time seeking sexual activities," said the demon. "Obtaining sex was difficult sometimes because women wanted to be loved for themselves, not for their bodies. When men couldn't find women who could be used, they channeled their sexual energies into other areas—into the arts, politics, business, but mostly aggressive behavior. Combined with depression, sexism can make godlike mankind the way we want to see it! Our race will discover its true talents! Our race will conquer the stars!"

"But how can it help me?" asked the lawyer.

"That's easy!" said the demon. "Sexism begins at home! Go to Kitty right now and tell her that you want to dip your wand into the sweet nectar of her honeypot, and that she'd better like it. Tell her she'll be happy because you're a male, because your body is equipped to make her happy! And don't let her doubt it! Make her succumb to the passions she'll feel. She'll feel them because you'll *tell* her to!"

The lawyer picked up his sword-cane and twirled it. He sent the mud on his suit to the anti-matter universe. "You're right! It'll work! I know it will! I've waited years for this!" He ran out of the room. His mind was full of visions of Kitty at the height of ecstasy.

The demon rubbed his hands in joy. "Now we have something to do! This is a task worthy of our talents!"

"Friend demon, we shall have fun doing this. Already I am becoming dissatisfied with my celibate life."

"Are you going to try to win back your wife?"

"Certainly not! There are hundreds of pretty godlike women I would like to make a carnal acquaintance with. We must set an example for the rest of godlike mankind."

The demon said, "I'll have to change my appearance so my body will be the proper size." He created paper and charcoal and began sketching designs for a new appearance. "And I'll have to learn how to ejaculate again."

"I am sure you will find that no problem." The fat man stood up. "As for myself, I will have to get into the proper physical condition." He did several deep knee-bends. "Tell me, friend demon, do you think the godlike women will like the way I strut my stuff?"

"If they don't, we're going to be shit out of fresh ideas," said the demon, sketching away frantically as the hailstones thundered down outside.

HARLAN ELLISON

"Here's a man who slams his work edge-on into your guts. You'll relish even the bruises. And it's long past time for Harlan Ellison to be awarded the title: 20th-century Lewis Carroll."

Philip José Farmer in the
Los Angeles Times

HE-4